NO GUN, NO HOPE

Skye heard the swish behind him, twisted away. But the lance struck him and he pitched forward over the horse's neck as the pain exploded in his shoulder. When he hit the ground, lights flashed in his eyes and he lost his grip on his rifle. Skye lay still until suddenly he felt another sharp stab of pain and stared up at Red Buffalo's massive head. The tip of the lance touched Skye's throat and he automatically pressed his arm against the holster. It was empty. . . .

THE TRAILSMAN

108

PAWNEE BARGAIN

by

Jon Sharpe

A SIGNET BOOK

SIGNET
Published by the Penguin Group
Penguin Books USA Inc., 375 Hudson Street,
New York, New York 10014, U.S.A.
Penguin Books Ltd, 27 Wrights Lane,
London W8 5TZ, England
Penguin Books Australia Ltd, Ringwood,
Victoria, Australia
Penguin Books Canada Ltd, 2801 John Street,
Markham, Ontario, Canada L3R 1B4
Penguin Books (N.Z.) Ltd, 182-190 Wairau Road,
Auckland 10, New Zealand

Penguin Books Ltd, Registered Offices:
Harmondsworth, Middlesex, England

First published by Signet, an imprint of New American Library,
a division of Penguin Books USA Inc.

First Printing, December, 1990
10 9 8 7 6 5 4 3 2 1

The first chapter of this book originally appeared in *Gunsmoke Gulch*, the
one hundred and seventh volume in this series.

 REGISTERED TRADEMARK—MARCA REGISTRADA

Printed in the United States of America

PUBLISHER'S NOTE
This is a work of fiction. Names, characters, places, and incidents either are the
product of the author's imagination or are used fictitiously, and any resemblance
to actual persons, living or dead, events, or locales is entirely coincidental.

The Trailsman

Beginnings . . . they bend the tree and they mark the man. Skye Fargo was born when he was eighteen. Terror was his midwife, vengeance his first cry. Killing spawned Skye Fargo, ruthless, cold-blooded murder. Out of the acrid smoke of gunpowder still hanging in the air, he rose, cried out a promise never forgotten.

The Trailsman, they began to call him, all across the West: searcher, scout, hunter, the man who could see where others only looked, his skills for hire but not his soul, the man who lived each day to the fullest, yet trailed each tomorrow. Skye Fargo, the Trailsman, the seeker who could take the wildness of a land and the wanting of a woman and make them his own.

*1860, the Colorado Territory
west of Pawnee Butte, where a man's life
could be measured by how careful he was . . .*

1

As Skye Fargo rode toward the big house at the end of town, he felt misgivings and curiosity swirling within him, each elbowing the other. The mixture had been there since the morning when the woman had halted him on the street. But curiosity had won out, he admitted to himself as he swung from the saddle and walked to the door of the house. But not just curiosity, he corrected himself. He had picked up the scent of a possible evening of pleasure.

Nothing defined, nothing had said as much, yet it was something one picked up when one had an educated nose for that sort of thing. Part experience, part intuition, but mostly it was a gift, he'd always felt—with a little smugness, he admitted.

His thoughts went back to the strangely intriguing conversation of the morning. He had arrived in Plainsville only the night before after breaking trail for a new wagon route for Bill Dunnellan. Finding a trail through the harshness of the Medicine Bow Range had been a slow, hard task and he'd welcomed the luxury of a good night's rest in a real bed at the town inn. He'd slept late and decided to give the Ovaro a thorough grooming after the weeks of hard trail riding: the dandy brush first, for the heavy dirt, caked mud, and sweat; the body brush to clean scruff from mane and tail; the stable rubber for a final polishing; and last, the hoof pick. He had just finished caring for the magnificent horse with its jet-black fore- and hind-quarters and pure white midsection when a woman had halted beside him.

He looked up to see her in an open-topped buckboard, and his lake-blue eyes swept over her in a glance that missed little. Still on the sunny side of forty, he guessed, but not by much, light-blue eyes, brown hair swept atop her head, a straight nose, and lips that were on the thin side. More than attractive enough, she had a face that bordered on brittleness, a hard edge to her good looks.

"You're Skye Fargo, the Trailsman," she said.

"Go to the head of the class," he returned. "You good at guessing or just lucky?"

"I was told you'd be arriving in Plainsville and I was given a description of your horse," she said, and swung down from the buckboard. "I'm Marilyn Evans." A blue blouse and skirt fitted close around a firm, tight little body without a trace of soft fat on it.

"Bill Dunnellan tell you I'd be arriving?" Fargo asked.

"No. He told Sheriff Hardesty, who told me. Seems the sheriff knew of you. You've a reputation," she said. Fargo waited as the woman's eyes moved appreciatively over his tall, muscled frame to linger on the chiseled contours of his face. "I've a job for you, Fargo. I hear you're the very best and that's what I want," Marilyn Evans said.

"Sorry, honey. No more jobs for now. Got some personal things to do," he told her.

"A special job with special pay," Marilyn Evans said.

"Sorry."

"I don't want to talk here," the woman said, ignoring his answer. "Come see me tonight. It'll be worth your while. I'll see to that."

He smiled. Words that really said very little but implied a lot. Promise or mere cleverness? He let the question slide through his mind as she stepped back into the buckboard. A very tight, trim rear, he noted.

She looked at him from the carriage, a note of cool imperiousness in her eyes. "I'll expect you tonight. The big house at the end of town. You can't miss it."

"I wouldn't wait up too late," he said.

Her eyebrows arched as she studied him for a long moment. "You leave me with two choices, Fargo," she said, and he waited. "I could have Sheriff Hardesty bring you," she said.

"You carry that much weight in this town, honey?" Fargo questioned.

"I do."

"You said two choices. What's the other one?"

"I could say please," she murmured.

He considered for a moment. "Try that," he remarked.

"Please," she said, the word delivered with just the right mixture of sincerity without pleading.

She was good, he thought. "No promises," he said.

She smiled as she drove away, and he watched her go with his eyes narrowed. He decided a visit to Bill Dunnellan was in order, but he found the man had left town for the day. His next stop was Sheriff Hardesty's office, where the sheriff turned out to be a paunchy, beefy-faced man with shifty eyes. He turned away almost every question with the remark: "Marilyn Evans is a fine woman."

"She wants me to do a job for her," Fargo said after a few moments of the bland answers, tossed the remark out to see if it drew anything better.

"Then I'd do it, mister," Hardesty said. "I'm sure she'll pay well."

"She seems to swing a lot of weight in this town," Fargo remarked.

"She's a fine woman," the sheriff said, retreating at once.

"She a widow lady?" Fargo asked. The sheriff's face stayed expressionless as he opened his mouth and Fargo cut him off. "I know, she's a fine woman," he grunted.

Sheriff Hardesty pulled his mouth closed as Fargo strode from the office. Fargo had met men such as Hardesty before. Some were bought and paid for. Others were afraid. Some merely knew what side their bread was buttered on. The end result was the same: men who'd deserted strength and independence.

He returned to the inn and relaxed during the rest of the day. But Marilyn Evans had certainly become more intriguing, and he knew then that curiosity would bring him to where he stood now, one hand upraised to knock at her door. A moment passed after his knock; he was about to knock again when the door opened and Marilyn Evans faced him in a silk jacquard dressing robe, an opulent garment that matched the regal look in her eyes. No surprise in her, he noted, and silently swore at her cool confidence.

"Please come in," she said, and led the way into a richly furnished living room with a tufted couch, a thick rug, and assorted invitingly deep armchairs. She lowered herself onto the couch beside a small table where a decanter of amber liquid and two glasses rested. "A drink?" she offered, and poured without waiting for an answer.

He sat down beside her, tasted the drink, and let the liquid circle his mouth. "Good. Tennessee sipping whiskey," he said approvingly.

"I expected you'd know your liquor," Marilyn Evans said, and leaned back. He saw modest breasts move under the silk robe. "I'm glad you decided to come by, Fargo," she said.

"Curiosity," he said

"About what I want you to do for me?"

"About you."

"They're tied together." She smiled. "My husband, Sam, ran away with Cindy, a little blond slut that worked as a dancer at the town dance hall. I want you to find them. I intend to bring him back." Fargo watched Marilyn Evans' face grow icy, the brittleness pushing hard against the attractiveness of her. "I'll pay you five hundred dollars," she finished.

"A powerful lot of money," he observed.

"I made Sam Evans into a name in this town. My money made him president of the bank. My money set him up in a feed business. My family's money turned him from a measly little clerk into a figure of power," she said.

"Why do I think the real power stayed in your hands?" Fargo remarked.

"That was between Sam and me. To the rest of the world he was an important man," Marilyn said. "He's not going to make a laughingstock out of me. He's not going to make me into the rejected wife left behind."

"I take it you're not all upset because you love him so much," Fargo said blandly.

"Love's got nothing to do with it. Legally, he's my husband. He can sign away my money. He can borrow on our name. He can start putting things into her name. I'm not waiting for any of that to happen. I'm going after him, and you're the one who can find him for me?"

"Sorry, but I'm not much for chasing runaway husbands," Fargo said. "Besides, I've got personal business to tend to."

"It can wait, I'm sure," she snapped arrogantly.

"Not this."

"I'll make it a thousand dollars."

Fargo smiled. "Marilyn, honey, you've got to stop thinking that money can buy you everything. Sorry."

"What's so damn important you'll turn down that kind of money?"

"I'm afraid you wouldn't understand," he said. "But you satisfied my curiosity." He drained the drink and started to push to his feet.

"No, wait," Marilyn Evans said, her voice suddenly soft, all the anger and arrogance gone from it. He sat back and saw that her face had softened, too, her expression almost sheepish. "I did some more asking about you. I heard that money didn't pull on you the way it does most men. You're right, there are things beside money."

"There are," he agreed.

"Things that count as much," she said, and he nodded as she rose and faced him. Her hand went to the top of the robe, pulled at the silk, and the garment fell open. It slid from her shoulders and dropped to the floor. She wore nothing beneath it, and he found himself gazing at a smallish figure, but a body that was taut and trim, with the skin tone of a girl twenty years her junior. Modest breasts stood out, not a trace of a sag in their firmness, with small pink-brown tips on areolae of matching color. A narrow waist flared into nice hips; her skin was tight across a flat abdomen, and a neat little triangle, not terribly dark, pointed the way to shapely legs of firm thighs and well-molded calves. She stepped

14

forward, her light-blue eyes suddenly darkened. "I've just increased the offer," she murmured.

"You sure have," he said as her arms slid around his neck. She helped him unbutton shirt, drop his gun belt, and pull off trousers until his skin touched hers and he felt a tiny shiver go through her. She slid downward, onto the thick rug, and pulled him with her as her lips pressed his, opened at once, and moved hungrily while her hands fluttered up and down his muscled back. Her skin was as tight to the touch as to the eye, a steel-wire tautness to her.

She gave a tiny gasp as his hands moved over the firm, modest breasts. The pink-brown tips grew firm at once and he felt her leg move up and down over his groin, rubbing with a catlike sensuousness. His throbbing warmth touched her flat belly and she gave a tiny gasp. Her legs drew up at once, fell open, and she pressed against him, her flat belly rubbing almost feverishly.

The wire tautness of her skin was but an echo of her body, and he felt the explosive tension in her as her hands moved across his muscled frame, found his pulsating warmth, and tightened around him. "Oh, God, yes . . . oh, Jesus, give me, give me," Marilyn Evans breathed, and brought her pelvis up to him, pushed him against her, touched her darkness to him, and gave a tiny scream.

He straightened his body, pressed her back on the rug, and heard her hiss of disappointment, which ended in a soft cry as his mouth closed around one firm, modest breast and drew in deeply in against his tongue. As he caressed the tip, pushed it back and forth with his tongue, Marilyn gasped out little cries of delight, and once again he felt her legs rubbing up and down against him.

"Jesus, Fargo, come to me, damn, come to me,"

she breathed, and he smiled. The demanding arrogance was in her even now and he held back, continuing to pull and suck on her firm breasts. Her cries grew louder and rose in pitch.

His hand moved down, over the flat belly, through the small wiry nap, and cupped her wetness. She flung her legs apart, her hips upward. "Oh, Jesus, now, now," she cried out, but he still held back. Her hands had become fists that pounded against his ribs. He moved his hand, touched the satin wetness, and Marilyn Evans screamed, pleading as well as wanting in the sound now. He held her, pressed the walls. Her mouth against his chest left a mark of hot, wet breath. Her tight, trim thighs quivered now and the electricity of her erupted, not unlike invisible sparks, igniting his own mounting hunger. He turned, brought himself to her, slid forward, and Marilyn screamed out in pleasure. Her smallish body lifted him with it as she arched her back, hips pushing upward. She pumped with almost frantic abandon, quick, short motions, each accompanied by a high-pitched, equally short cry.

There was no slow pleasure in her, he realized. Instead, she was like a wildcat in a mating frenzy, the body beyond all control, the senses absolutely in command. He felt himself swept along with her. When her escalting cries suddenly erupted in a frenzied scream and he felt her thighs tighten against him, he let himself join her. "Oh, Jesus . . . aaaiiiiii . . . oh, Jesus," she screamed as the moment showered ecstasy and she trembled until, with the suddenness of a wire snapping, she went limp.

She fell back onto the rug and lay with her eyes closed, her breath coming in deep gasps, the modest breasts still quivering. He lay over her, stayed with her, and it took minutes before she pulled her eyes open. "Oh, my God . . . oh, my God," she murmured.

"You always this way or haven't you been to the well in a long time?" he asked as she stared up at him.

"Both," she answered, and moaned in protest as he pulled from her finally. He let her lie, gathering breath, and with the brittleness gone from her face, she was a right pretty women, he decided. Finally she sat up on one elbow, the firm breasts moving as one. "Convinced now it'll be worth your while?" she asked with a smug smile. "I'd say that's the right way to seal a bargain."

"It was real nice," Fargo said. "But I don't see it sealing anything."

She sat up straighter and a furrow came to her brow. "What do you mean?"

"It's still no, honey," he said, and shrugged apologetically.

"You bastard," Marilyn Evans hissed, and pulled her robe around herself. "Why'd you make love to me if you weren't going to agree? You know what that meant."

"Never look a gift horse in the mouth, my daddy always said," Fargo answered.

"Damn you, " she flung back, the hardness in her face again. "You're certainly no gentlemen."

"Maybe not. But you're sure as hell no lady," he said as he finished dressing. He started for the door and paused to look at her as she quivered in fury. "But thanks for a lovely evening," he said.

"You'll be sorry, Fargo," Marilyn Evans screamed after him.

"I've been sorry before," he said as he closed the door and strode into the night. He heard something shatter as it struck the door behind him. One of the glasses, he guessed as he walked over to the Ovaro and pulled himself into the saddle. Marilyn Evans was a demanding women, plainly used to getting her own way. In bed and out of it. Maybe this would teach her a lesson, he reflected.

He stopped at the public stable, secured a nice box stall for the pinto, and strolled to the inn, where he undressed in the dark and stretched out on the bed. One more night of luxury before returning to the trail, come morning, he reminded himself. Sleep came quickly as he enjoyed the softness of the mattress and pillow.

The night grew deeper and he was thoroughly wrapped in sleep when a splintering crash sent him leaping up in the bed. He dived for the gun belt he'd hung on the bedpost when a voice grated against his ears. "Don't try it, mister," it said, a vaguely familiar ring to it. Fargo froze in midair and slowly turned to see Sheriff Hardesty and two more men, all with guns trained on him, the smashed-in door hanging from one hinge behind them.

Fargo lowered his arm and sat back on the bed, his lake-blue eyes narrowed at the trio. They were too close to miss. "You always come calling like this?" he asked the sheriff

"Only when we have a real criminal," the man said, a sneer on his beefy face. "Get dressed, Fargo. You're going to jail."

"What for? I snore too loud?"

"Don't get smart with me," the sheriff growled.

Fargo's eyes narrowed as they bored into the man, and he felt the dark spiral of thought forming inside him. "What for?" he insisted again.

"For assaulting Marilyn Evans, that's what for," Sheriff Hardesty said, and Fargo felt the bitter satisfaction of his own suspicions.

"That's a crock of shit and you know it," Fargo snapped as he began to dress.

"All I know is what she said," Hardesty replied.

"And she's a fine woman," Fargo grunted bitterly.

"She is that." Hardesty nodded as Fargo finished dressing. "Leave the gun belt. We'll bring that along," the sheriff ordered, and Fargo found himself flanked by the two men, each with a six-gun poked into his ribs. He noted the deputy badges they wore as he walked from the room.

Outside, the sheriff led the way down the street the few hundred yards to the jail. "I've already sent for Judge Morris," he said. He pushed the office door open and Fargo saw the two cells in the back of the building. Hardesty put his Colt into the top drawer of a desk, Fargo noted as he was pushed farther into the room. He turned as the door opened and a small man, gray-haired with pince-nez glasses entered, his shirt open at the neck under his black frock coat.

"I take it this is him," the man said as he peered at Fargo and drew a piece of legal paper from inside his coat.

"That's him, Skye Fargo," Hardesty said.

"I'm Judge Morris, Fargo," the man said.

"No shit," Fargo bit out. "You want to get on with the rest of this goddamn charade."

The judge fastened a stern glance at him. "This is a serious charge," he intoned, holding up the piece of paper. "Marilyn Evans has charged you with forcing your way into her house and taking carnal liberties with her. That's a hanging charge, mister."

"That's a dammed lie, every bit of it," Fargo said. "Not that you give a damn."

"Are you accusing me of ignoring truth?" Judge Morris bellowed.

"Heaven forbid," Fargo said. "I'm just accusing you of taking orders."

The judge's face reddened and he pushed the piece of paper back into his pocket. "I can't fit this into my trial calendar for at least a month," he said to Hardesty. "Meanwhile he stays under lock and key." He yanked the door open and stormed into the darkness.

"In there," Hardesty said, and motioned to the first of the two cells. Fargo entered the small cubicle, a single cot along one wall and the sheriff slammed the barred door after him. "I'm leaving Timmy, here, in charge for the night," Hardesty said with a nod to the younger of the two deputies. "My advice to you, mister, is to stop accusing people around here."

"Thanks for caring," Fargo said.

"Go to hell," Hardesty snapped, and strode from the jail, the other deputy following. The younger man went to the small desk at the front of the jail and Fargo lowered himself to the edge of the cot. Not more than five minutes had passed when the office door opened and Marilyn Evans entered.

"Wait outside, Timmy," she said, and the deputy hurried out.

"Been wondering how long it would be before you showed up." Fargo smiled as he rose, and she walked to the cell. Prudently, she halted a few feet from the bars.

"I told you you'd be sorry," she said.

"I'm not sorry—not yet, anyway."

"What makes you so damn stubborn?" she flung at him.

"I've something to do and I'm going to do it, simple as that."

"You won't do it sitting in this jail cell."

"We'll see." He smiled.

"You'll come around."

"We'll see," he said, and smiled again as she

spun on her heel and strode from the jail. She did have a beautifully trim little rear, he noted again. And he'd underestimated her ruthless determination. He wouldn't do that again. But she'd said one true thing: he couldn't do what he had to do sitting in this cell.

The Trailsman watched the young deputy return and sit down at the desk. Lowering himself to the edge of the cot, Fargo let his hand slowly steal down his leg to the double-bladed throwing knife in the calf holster.

ers. His eyes moved to the girl. Her dark eyes
were fixed on him with intense concentration. She
were that the chair beside his when Fargo moved
forward, as Timmy raise the rifle again, moved and
stepped back, and . . . thick as . . . been in . . . to . . .

2

Fargo kept his gaze fixed on the deputy at the desk
as he silently drew the thin, double-edged blade
from its calf holster. Timmy leaned back in his
chair, thoroughly relaxed, certain that his prisoner
was safely confined to the cell.

The Trailsman slipped the blade into his belt
behind his back where he could have it in hand in a
split second. But he grimaced as he peered at the
deputy. It would be easy to send the throwing knife
hurling through the cell bars and into Timmy. But
that would avail him nothing. The man would be
dead at his desk and he'd still be behind bars, Fargo
grunted silently. He had to bring the man close.
Besides, he didn't want any killing. Timmy was no
more than a hired hand, paid to do a job. Fargo
thought for a few moments and then rose to his
feet.

"There's no damn place to go in here," he shouted,
and saw the deputy turn to look at him and slowly
rise to his feet. Fargo swore inwardly as he saw the
man take a rifle from a wall case.

"Get back from the door," Timmy ordered as he
began to walk toward him.

Fargo obeyed at once and watched the man hold
the rifle in the crook of his arm as he took a large
key ring from his pocket and put one of the keys
into the cell-door lock. Fargo waited, his every mus-

cle tensed, but the rifle was still trained fully on him. Even if the deputy fired in haste, the chances were that the shot couldn't miss, and Fargo moved forward as Timmy swung the cell door open and stepped back.

"Over there," the man said, and motioned to a back corner of the jail where a narrow wooden door marked the toilet. Fargo walked to the facility and saw the deputy keep his distance. He had been trained well.

Fargo entered the toilet and pulled the door closed behind him. The deputy would continue to keep his distance and the rifle trained on him when he came out, Fargo realized, and he grimaced as he let thoughts race through his mind. This would be his only chance and he drew the knife from behind his back inside the toilet. He let the minutes tick off in silence and finally heard Timmy's voice.

"Get out of there. You've had enough time," the man called.

Fargo remained silent as he faced the narrow door, the thin knife in one hand. He let another few minutes pass and the deputy called out again, the hint of apprehension in his voice. "Dammit, get the hell out of there," Timmy called. Again Fargo remained silent. "Goddamn, you come out of there." The deputy shouted, but now an edge of alarm had come into his voice.

Fargo stayed silent, every muscle tensed as he heard Timmy start toward the door. The man would yank the door open, he knew, but the space was too confined, the door too narrow for him to pull it open without turning the rifle aside for a second. That second was all Fargo would need. His eyes were fastened on the door as it was yanked open. The rifle was deflected for an instant and the deputy flew backward as the battering ram of muscle, bone, and sinew hurtled into him.

Fargo's one hand closed around the rifle barrel and forced it downward while his other hand pressed the knife against Timmy's throat. "Drop the rifle," he hissed, the knife-edge drawing a trickle of blood from the man's throat. Fargo heard the clatter of the rifle hitting the floor, and he yanked the man's six gun from its holster and pushed Timmy away. Fear stayed in the man's face as Fargo flicked a glance to the cell to see that the keys were still in the door. He gestured with the revolver. "Get in the cell," he ordered. "Don't make me do anything I don't want to do."

The deputy obeyed, backing into the cell through the open door. Fargo slammed the door shut and pulled the key from the lock. He considered gagging the man but decided against it. It would delay him, and the jail walls were thick, the cell in the rear. It was unlikely anyone would hear him shout.

Fargo tossed the key ring on the desk along with the man's gun and retrieved his own Colt and gun belt, paused to look back at Timmy. "Enjoy yourself. Hardesty will be around in the morning, I'm sure," he said, and strode from the jail.

He waited outside the door and listened. No sound penetrated to the outside. He hurried down the dark night streets to the stable. He found the Ovaro in a rear stall and his eyes went to the saddle pegs along one wall. He found his tack and was reaching out to take it down when a voice cut in.

"Surprise," the voice said. "Hold it right there, mister."

Fargo turned to see the other deputy and another man, both with rifles trained on him.

"Drop your gun, nice and slow," the deputy ordered, and Fargo carefully lifted the Colt out of its

24

holster and dropped it on the floor. He swore silently as initial surprise turned to chagrin. "Step back," the deputy said, and scooped up the Colt as Fargo moved away from it. "Get the sheriff, Tom. Quick," the deputy said, and the other man ran from the stable. "Goddamn, she was right," the man said with a kind of admiration in his voice.

"Who was right?" Fargo asked.

"Mrs. Evans," the deputy said.

"Right about what?" Fargo queried, and the man didn't reply as the running footsteps resounded and Sheriff Hardesty burst into the stable to stare at him.

"I'll be damned. She was right," the sheriff said.

"That seems to be everybody's opinion, whatever it means," Fargo said, and heard the bitterness in his voice.

"She said you were the kind to escape and that you'd take out anyone we had at the jail," Hardesty said. "But the first thing you'd do is come for your horse so we ought to keep a watch on him."

"Is that what she said?"

"I didn't rightly believe her, but damn, she was right," Hardesty said. "Goddamn, she's one smart lady."

"And a fine woman," Fargo bit out as he silently cursed Marilyn Evans. She wasn't smart. But she was canny and shrewd, and he'd find a way to deal with that.

The sheriff's voice broke into his thoughts.

"You kill Timmy, damn you?"

"He's locked in the cell," Fargo said.

"Take him back," Hardesty ordered the others, and Fargo stayed silent as he was marched back to the jail. The younger deputy had the decency to look embarrassed when he was let out.

"He had a damn knife on him," he said, and nodded to Fargo.

"Search him," Hardesty ordered, and it took the two men only a minute to find the calf holster and the double-edged blade. "You won't be pulling any more stunts now," the sheriff snapped as they returned Fargo to the cell and locked the door. But as a precaution, Hardesty had two of his men stay the night.

Fargo lay down on the cot, stretched his long, powerful frame out beyond the cot's limits, and let his thoughts begin to form themselves into a plan.

Marilyn would visit in the morning. He was certain of that. She'd gloat, play the victor, even though she knew the hollowness of the role. She needed him. Keeping him in jail wouldn't help her any more than it would him. Under the victor's cloak she'd be desperately hoping he'd give in. He'd do exactly that, he had already decided, but when the moment was right. First, he would take her on an emotional seesaw, from fury to frustration, reason to relief. When he agreed, she'd be too relieved to question anything he said. He managed a grim smile as he turned on his side and let sleep sweep over him.

When morning came, he was allowed out to go to the toilet and then wash out of a large bucket brought into the cell. Breakfast was coffee and a hard roll that tasted unexpectedly good. He relaxed on the cot afterward and Hardesty arrived to take over for the two deputies.

Fargo estimated it was about noon when Marilyn Evans strode into the jail and he swung from the cot to offer her a smile. "The clever Mrs. Evans," he said.

"Wait outside," she snapped at Hardesty, and the man hurriedly left.

"It must be nice to have people scurry at your every word," Fargo remarked.

The brittleness was in her face as she fixed him with a stony glance. "You ready to come to your senses?"

"Meaning what?"

"You know damn well what," she hissed.

"Sorry." He shrugged almost apologetically and lowered himself to the edge of the cot.

"Dammit, Fargo! What could you possibly have to do that'd make you turn down everything I've offered?" she flung at him, exasperation in her voice. "What's so damn important?"

"You wouldn't understand."

"Try me. What in hell is it that you have to do?" Marilyn frowned.

It was time for part of the truth, Fargo decided. "I've got to go to a birthday party," he said.

Marilyn Evans' jaw dropped, and he heard her breath suck in as she stared at him, her face flooding with incredulousness. "A birthday party?" she echoed, the words emerging in a hoarse croak.

"That's right." He smiled affably.

The incredulousness in her face gave way to livid rage. "You bastard. You rotten, stinking bastard. You can rot in here until they hang you," she shouted and stormed from the jail.

Hardesty reentered, cast an uncertain glance at him, and Fargo lay back and stretched out on the cot. He made a wager with himself, and he won: the day had not come to an end when Marilyn stormed back into the jailhouse. Hardesty left without being told to, this time, Fargo noted with a smile as the woman faced him through the bars, hands on her hips.

"You don't really expect I'd believe that cock-and-bull birthday party story, do you?" she accused.

"Why not? It's the truth," he said, and rose from the cot.

"What kind of a birthday party?" Marilyn demanded.

Fargo smiled again inwardly. It was time to give her the rest of the truth and let reasonability frustrate her this time.

"A party for a wonderful woman, Agatha Benson. She was a real friend to my pa and ma when I was little, and to me, too. She's a selfless, saintly woman, and when she left our town, I promised I'd be at her hundreth birthday. Well, she made it to a hundred and there's going to be a party for her. I've still time to make it."

"How touching," Marilyn said. "And you're passing up everything I offered you for an old lady's hundredth birthday party. That's got to be the dumbest damn reason I ever heard."

"Probably is, but it's mine and I'm staying with it," Fargo answered.

"You won't be at any damn birthday party," Marilyn exploded. "You'll be sitting right here till they hang you. You won't be escaping again."

He frowned at her and let his face grow clouded as he seemed bothered by her words and he saw the satisfaction in her eyes. "You won't be chasing down your husband either," he muttered.

"I'll hire somebody else," she said, and turned away to stride to the door. Even in angry, pounding footsteps, her firm, tight little rear hardly moved, he noted.

"Better hurry up on it," he called as she reached the door. "You've got a cold trail now and it's getting colder every day."

She flung a furious glance at him as she slammed the door shut.

He lowered himself onto the cot and smiled. Half the emotional seesaw was in full swing, fury and frustration. The other half, reason and relief, would come next. But he had to force himself to wait, though time was beginning to press on him. He had to let her stew long enough . . .

He turned thoughts from Marilyn Evans to Agatha Benson. Much warmer thoughts. He smiled. Agatha had lived the past ten years in a little town called Bent Arrow right on the border of the Colorado and Wyoming territories. He still had time to reach the town, given a fair amount of luck. Agatha's niece had written him of the celebration almost a year ago, and he looked forward to seeing some other old friends she'd told him would be there.

Agatha's niece, herself past fifty, was another strong woman who'd outlived two husbands in carving a home in the middle of unfriendly territory. It had been Agatha's own strength that had been such a bulwark to his father and mother in those years that seemed more distant than they really were. Appearing at her hundreth birthday was not just a gesture but a pilgrimage of respect and gratitude, not unlike paying an old debt. The likes of Marilyn Evans were sure as hell not going to keep him from that.

After a supper of lukewarm gruel and hard bread he let himself fall asleep until morning dawned.

After washing and shaving, with Hardesty and one of his deputies at the front desk, he called out. The time had come to move forward. "Tell Marilyn I want to see her," he said with just the right amount of sullenness in his voice.

"You heard what the man said," Hardesty barked, and the deputy ran from the jail. The sheriff stepped outside and waited for Marilyn to arrive. She entered with a combination of hope and hostility in her face. He let her come to the cell bars and stand there for a moment before he rose.

"You come to your senses?" she asked as hope broke through the hostility.

"I figure this is a Chinese stand off," he said. "As you put it, honey, I can't make my birthday party sitting in here." He paused and watched the excitement spiral in her face. "And you know there's nobody else that has a chance of finding your husband except me," he said. He paused again and let it appear as though it were difficult for him to form the words.

"Go on," she said, satisfaction quick to surface.

"I figure I've no choice but to find your damn husband and hope I've time left to reach my party," he said truculently.

"At last," Marilyn Evans said.

"One thing, though. We hit the trail, we do things my way. No second guessing, no arguments."

"Fine. You're the best. Whatever you say goes," she agreed. She shouted for Hardesty, and the sheriff came in. "Let him out," she ordered, and the cell door was unlocked at once. "Give him his gear," she said, and Hardesty returned the Colt and the calf-holster with the blade. "Tell Judge Morris I'm dropping all charges," Marilyn said as Fargo strapped on the calf holster and followed her from the jail.

"We've some talking to do," he said to her. "You ought to know there's no way I can pick up a trail this cold on the ground. I need some kind of lead where your husband and his girlfriend may have gone."

"I have that," Marilyn said. "He knew one route out of Plainsville. He used to drive it when he sold pots and pans."

"Before he met you," Fargo said, and she nodded.

"It's due north from here, toward Wyoming. It's

the only way he'd know to start. Of course, God knows where he's gone now."

"Leave that to me. There are some trading posts and small towns up that way," Fargo said. "You have any idea how they're traveling?"

"Somebody saw them leave. Two horses and a packhorse," she said, and he nodded, his eyes narrowed in thought.

"He could wind up in Indian country that way."

"Sam's no hero. He'd avoid that," she said. Fargo discarded a reply, then another, settled on a third.

"Maybe he'll think that's exactly what you'd figure," he pushed at her.

"He's not that smart," she said, and Fargo swore silently.

"Makes no difference. Maybe cutting through Indian country will be a shortcut for us," he said. Her lips pursed and he blew a silent sigh as she accepted the answer. "There anyplace to buy casks of whiskey here in town?" he asked.

"The dance hall," she said.

"Get a wagon—a farm wagon or a berry wagon will do," he said. "Load it with casks of whiskey. Then have the casks covered all around with a tarpaulin so nobody will know what we're hauling."

"What's all this for?" Marilyn queried.

"It's easier to buy your way through Indian country than fight your way through."

She kept the frown as she answered. "Whatever you say. Meet me at the house in an hour."

"I'll be there," he said, and smiled inside himself as he watched her hurry away. So far so good, he told himself as he strolled to the stable. Her relief at his capitulation was the major factor in keeping her probing, naturally suspicious mind in check, exactly as he'd planned. But he couldn't grow careless. She was too sharp for that, he reminded himself.

If he hadn't reminded himself, Marilyn did it for him when he arrived at her place. The wagon, an old Owensboro rack bed, hitched to a team of heavy-legged horses, had the tarpaulin tightly wrapped around its cargo. Five men on horseback waited alongside the wagon with Marilyn on a dark-gray mare.

"I hired these men some time ago," she said to Fargo. "I thought Sam might not come back willingly. Now they'll also be protection in Indian country." She introduced him to the five men, all drifters willing to hire out for anything, he decided, and he didn't even bother to memorize their names. They'd not be riding together too long.

"Ready to roll?" he asked Marilyn. She nodded yes and one of the five men took the reins of the wagon team.

Fargo led the way from town and turned north. Marilyn stayed beside him, her hired hands riding alongside the wagon. The Trailsman rode wrapped in his own thoughts as he reviewed his plans. First and foremost was General Sherwood Leeds, Commander of the Fifth Division United States Cavalry and an old friend. Fargo had worked for and with the general on many occasions and he knew the general kept a permanent field headquarters along the banks of the South Platte just below Horsetooth in the Colorado Territory.

But he couldn't just ride directly to the general's encampment. He had to be circuitous, make the planned seem unplanned, the premeditated a matter of luck. Anything else would raise Marilyn's suspicious nature at once. She was overjoyed and relieved he'd given in to her, but she wasn't ready to offer real trust. The five hired hands behind him were further proof of that.

He finished reviewing his next moves, and when

the day ended, they were in the high plains. He chose a place to camp beside a small stream. Supper was cold buffalo jerky and coffee heated over a tiny fire.

Marilyn paused beside him as he started to move from the site with his bedroll.

"Where are you going?" She frowned.

"Off by myself. I most always do."

"Why?"

"Different reasons. Sometimes to keep my own watch. Sometimes to make sure I'm not caught with everybody else if something unexpected happens," he told her.

"Sleep well," she said.

He moved on, but he glanced back and saw her talking to the other men where they had begun to bed down. Fargo smiled as he strolled on. She was arranging to keep him under watch. Four-hour shifts most likely. That way everyone would be rested enough to ride, come morning. He wasn't at all surprised. But he bedded down some hundred yards upstream and went to sleep satisfied.

When morning came, bright and warm, he shifted direction to the northwest.

"Why?" Marilyn questioned at once.

"There's a way station for mail riders some fifteen miles from here. It has a feed-and-supply store along with it. Many travelers going through these parts stop there," he said.

"Sam might have," Marilyn murmured. "Sounds worth a try."

He nodded and led the way in a wide circle that eventually took them southward. He found himself scanning the horizon and the closer rises of land with increasing frequency as he saw more and more unshod pony prints. All small parties, he noted, probably hunting for game. But then it could be scalps, he knew all too well. He shot a glance at Marilyn from time to time and saw she was holding up very well as he set a pace with a few stops to rest.

She had relaxed more, the lines of tension gone from her face and her natural attractiveness restored.

Fargo slowed when they came in sight of the way station, a huddle of three ramshackle buildings. "You all move on past. Keep going south. I'll go in alone," he said, and drew an immediate frown from Marilyn. "You've got to understand the men who run these way stations. They don't stay around long if they're loose-lipped. The fellow that runs this one knows me. I can get him to open up but not if there's somebody else there," he explained, and she nodded in understanding. He put the pinto into a canter and left her and the others, reined to a halt at the doorway of the way station, and swung to the ground. He glanced back to see Marilyn and the others moving slowly past.

The man inside the station, a lanky figure in a torn undershirt that had once been white and loose-hanging trousers, had an old Hawkens plains rifle across the counter. "Howdy," he said as Fargo entered.

"Afternoon." Fargo nodded. "Could use an extra canteen and the water to fill it."

"Fifty cents for the canteen, five cents for the water," the man said, and proceeded to fill a burlap-covered canteen with water from a tall jar.

"Been seeing a lot of Indian pony prints," Fargo remarked.

"Too goddamn many," the man grunted.

"They give you trouble?"

"Not usually," the man answered. "They use the station the way a mountain lion uses a water hole."

Fargo's smile was grim, the man's words graphic

to those who knew the ways of the mountain lion. Like the water hole to the big cat, the station was a magnet to be left alone but used to pick out and then track a likely quarry.

"Luck to you, friend," Fargo said, paid the man, and returned to the Ovaro.

Marilyn and the wagon were tiny shapes down the plains, but he quickly caught up to them and swung in alongside her. "We got lucky," he said, and watched the excitement flood her face. "He stopped there with his girlfriend. The station master remembered her best. They told him they were heading south, and that means we're in even more luck."

"How so?" Marilyn asked.

"General Sherwood Leeds is an old friend of mine. His field headquarters is due south of here. We'll stop by and see him," Fargo said.

"Why? I doubt Sam would be stopping at any army post," Marilyn said.

"Probably not, but General Leeds has patrols covering every mile of the territory around him. Chances are damn good that one of them saw Sam and the girl," Fargo said. "They'd stop and see if everything was all right, just as a matter of courtesy."

"And they'd report that back to the general," Marilyn said, excitement curling in her voice.

"Exactly. They report back on everything," Fargo said. "That means we'd have a really fresh lead."

"Let's go," Marilyn said, and returned his expansive smile. "When will we reach the general's camp?" she asked.

"Tomorrow," he said as he saw the shadows of dusk beginning to slide over the land.

The terrain grew more hilly, black oak clustered in thick stands along with red cedar. He found a place to camp in a thicket of oak, and when the others were settled down, he took his bedroll and climbed up onto a low ridge that let him see across the moonlit terrain below. He had undressed and stretched out on his bedroll when he heard a rustle of brush. He sat up, the Colt in his hand instantly. He listened to the sound and smiled as he put the gun down and waited.

Finally, Marilyn's trim, smallish shape came into sight, paused, peered in one direction and then another, and finally spotted him. She hurried forward and he saw she had a robe wrapped around herself. She halted beside him and he gazed at her with his face set.

"What are you doing up here?" he questioned.

"Come looking for you," she said, and dropped to her knees beside him.

"You figure to make everything all right?" he asked, putting a note of hurt into his voice.

"I don't think our little disagreement back in town ought to stand in the way of anything else," she said.

He let himself consider her answer for a moment and then he smiled as he reached up for her. "I guess not," he said, and she fell against him, the robe coming open and the firm, smallish breasts falling onto his chest. Her skin was warm, its tight smoothness exciting. Her mouth found his with instantly hungry fervor. It would be the icing on the cake, he told himself as he pressed her hands across her breasts and felt her quiver, gasp, and cry out in delight. She tried to be in command, as she had the first time, but again he refused her that and heard her ecstasy through her protest as he teased, caressed, quickened and slowed, and quickened again until she writhed and cried out in desperate wanting.

When he carried her to the very brink and finally

over it, Marilyn Evans screamed into his chest while her fist struck his shoulders, every inch of her tight, taunt body consumed by senses. Her cries finally trailed off in sputtering gasps. She clung to him as ecstasy slowly receded, the flesh trying to cling to that which was beyond clinging.

Finally she lay against him, her breath returning to normal. She brought the willful ruthlessness that was part of her to making love and imparted its òwn kind of excitement, a draining, hard-edged quality where tenderness played no part. He had taken her on her own terms and enjoyed doing it. She deserved no more, and he found himself feeling sympathy for Sam Evans.

Marilyn pushed up on one elbow, a tight little smile of anticipation toying with her lips. "Tomorrow we get a real lead on that little runaway bastard and his floozie," she said. "I'm really looking forward to tomorrow."

"Me, too." Fargo smiled.

3

In the morning, Marilyn was plainly excited as they rode south, but it was late afternoon before Fargo came into sight of the field headquarters camp. A double row of barrack tents stretched out on both sides of a large, main-headquarters tent, the brown army mounts tethered in a line on both sides of the camp. He saw a section of the area marked for drilling and training, another for recreation, everything neat and disciplined in true army fashion. The regimental flag flew at the top of the large main tent, and two rows of sentries watched the visitors with rifles at the ready.

Fargo steered the Ovaro toward the big tent and reined to a halt when a sergeant stepped forward. "State your business, mister," the noncom said.

"Come to see General Leeds," Fargo told him.

"Name?"

"Fargo," the Trailsman said, and the sergeant strode into the main tent.

"The general runs a tight ship," Fargo muttered to Marilyn, and swung to the ground as he saw the tall, ramrod straight figure hurry from the tent, gold-trimmed blue uniform crisply pressed as always.

"By God, Fargo, this is some kind of miracle," General Leeds roared, and followed with a hearty handshake. "I've been trying to reach you for the last month."

"I've got misgivings already," Fargo said, and drew a laugh from the tall, straight figure. "You haven't changed any, General," Fargo said as he took in the strong face, long nose and sharp blue eyes, a face much younger than the shock of white hair indicated. "This is Mrs. Marilyn Evans," he introduced, and the general acknowledged his words with a click of his heels and a quick bow.

"My pleasure, General," Marilyn said in her sweetest voice.

"What brings you visiting us?" General Leeds asked her.

"Fargo has some questions," she said.

"Good. I've things to talk to him about," the general said. He tossed a quick glance at the wagon and the other men before returning his eyes to Marilyn. "We keep some tents for unexpected guests. The sergeant will take you and your people to them. You can rest, freshen up or whatever while Fargo and I talk," he said, and returned to the big tent with a polite nod.

"I'll come by later," Fargo said to Marilyn.

"Don't forget what we're here for," she reminded him.

"Trust me," Fargo said, and watched Marilyn and the others follow the sergeant down the line of tents. When he went into the main tent, he found General Leeds behind a small table in a corner that almost resembled a proper office with a tall cardboard file cabinet and a territory map hung onto a wired support. Fargo lowered himself into one of three straight-backed chairs as the general fastened him with a reflective smile.

"It's been a while, old friend," Leeds said.

"It has," Fargo agreed.

"But stories about you kept reaching me. They were reassuring," the general said, and Fargo frowned at the last words. "They told me you were still alive and still doing things most men only think about," Leeds explained. "I've a job for you, Fargo."

"I don't need a job. I don't want a job, especially not one of yours," Fargo said. "I'm on my way somewhere."

"For the woman with you?"

"No, something else," Fargo said.

"Hear me out," General Leeds said.

"Do I have a choice?" Fargo asked wryly, and received a shrug in return. The general had the power to command the services of any civilian in the territory, Fargo knew, and he was the man to invoke it if he had to.

"There is trouble in the Medicine Bow country," the general said. "Into the range and all around it."

"The Cheyenne?" Fargo inquired.

"Maybe, but my reports say the Pawnee," General Leeds answered. "I don't have any details, but I don't like the reports I'm getting, mostly from old scouts and trappers. Washington sent a new man up there to the stockade just south of Horse Creek. You know the place." Fargo nodded and the general went on, rising from his chair to pace back and forth, "His name's Duvall, Major Duvall. I've sent couriers up there for reports but he's playing games with me. He sends back answers that cover only minor details and imply that everything's just fine. But I keep hearing very differently."

"He afraid you'll yank him?"

"Maybe. More likely he's dragging his feet because he knows I objected to his assignment with Washington."

"Why?"

"That's powder-keg country. He's strictly book-trained, out of an office job, no real field experience and certainly no understanding of the Indian.

From what I'm hearing, he's doing more to create trouble than to keep things calm," General Leeds said. "I don't want a full-fledged Indian war with the tribes on the warpath, and I can't take my troopers and go charging up there and leave the whole southern territory unprotected, not unless I've a solid reason to go. Washington would have my scalp otherwise."

"I can finish the speech for you," Fargo said. "And I told you I've personal things to do."

"This is more important," Leeds said. "I want you to get up there, find out what's going on, and stop it if you can. If you can't, you report back to me. Now what about this Marilyn Evans and the others you're with?"

Fargo didn't answer as his thoughts raced. The general had added a new dimension to the situation, but it didn't really change his plan in coming here. He could go ahead with that much, anyway, Fargo mused, and argue further with the general later. He brought his eyes back to Sherwood Leeds and saw the faintly bemused expression in the man's face. The general was a hard man to fool. They had worked together too often, Fargo reminded himself.

"She hired me to track down her runaway husband and his girlfriend," Fargo said.

"Doesn't seem like your kind of pie, old friend," Leeds commented.

"She about owns a town called Plainsville. She had me over a barrel," Fargo said. "But I found out that what she's really doing is smuggling whiskey to the Indians. The runaway husband was an excuse. That wagon's loaded with whiskey casks."

He saw the surprise come into General Leeds' strong face. "She doesn't look the type to run whiskey," the general observed carefully.

"Looks can be deceiving," Fargo said.

"So can some people when they've a mind to," Leeds returned blandly.

"Look in the wagon," Fargo said with a hurt note in his voice. "You'll find it full of whiskey casks."

"I'm sure it will be," the general said.

"She'll deny it, of course. God knows what she'll say. She might even claim I told her to bring the whiskey."

"Wouldn't surprise me if she said exactly that." The general smiled, returning Fargo's bland innocence, and Fargo swore silently at the old fox and knew he was having difficulty keeping his own expression of earnest sincerity. "Now let me guess," Leeds said. "You think I ought to arrest her and the others and hold them, right?"

"That's what you do to people running whiskey to the Indians, don't you?" Fargo asked.

"That's what we do." The general nodded, leaned back, his lips pursed in thought. He returned his eyes to Fargo after a moment. "The world is made of bargains—accommodations, you might call them," he said philosophically. "How about this one? I arrest your gang of whiskey-runners and you go to the Medicine Bow Range?"

Fargo swore inwardly. It wasn't turning out exactly as he'd planned. He wanted to go his way free and clear. But he knew he hadn't fooled Sherwood Leeds for even a half-minute. The bargain was the best he could expect, he reckoned. Half a loaf was better than none. "Agreed." he said grimly, and the general smiled back.

"The usual army special-duty scout pay," Leeds said.

"Slave labor," Fargo muttered.

The general took his quill pen and a sheet of official army stationary and began to write in a bold hand. "I'll give you a letter of credentials from me.

Major Duvall can't ignore you, then," he said, and when he finished, Fargo put the short message into his pocket and followed Leeds from the tent. "Bring ten troopers," the general barked at the sergeant, slowed, and waited for the man to return with the ten rifle-bearing troopers.

Leeds led the small procession to where the wagon had been pulled alongside one of the tents, the five hired hands nearby. Marilyn stepped from the tent and swept the general and Fargo in a quick glance with the edge of a frown in it. "Take the tarp off that wagon," the general ordered.

"What is this?" Marilyn cut in, the frown very much on her brow now.

General Leeds ignored her as he watched the tarpaulin come off and the neat rows of whiskey casks come into view. "Put these people under guard," he ordered, and the troopers moved instantly to disarm the five men.

"What's this all about?" Marilyn questioned as she stepped forward.

"It's about selling whiskey to the Indians. Fargo told me what was under that tarpaulin. You're all under arrest," the general said sternly.

"Goddammit, he told me to bring all that whiskey," Marilyn protested.

"Ridiculous," Fargo scoffed.

"But he did," Marilyn said to the general.

"You'll get a chance to tell your story to a proper military court, soon as I can get one together," Leeds answered.

"Dammit, the whiskey was all his idea," Marilyn shouted.

"Why would I bring a wagonload of whiskey along to go chasing a runaway husband?" Fargo asked.

"No reason I can see," the general said as he

turned away. "Leg irons," he said to the sergeant, and quickly strode off.

"Dammit, you come back here," Marilyn shouted after Leeds, but the general had already receded into the darkness. The troopers began to shepherd the five men away from the wagon, and Fargo walked to the Ovaro and pulled himself into the saddle. "You bastard," Marilyn shouted at him as she followed. "You stinking, rotten son of a bitch. You planned this. You set this up."

Fargo smiled at her. "I seem to remember sitting in that jail on your trumped-up charges," he said. "And you'd have let me stay there. But that's a game two can play, honey. See you around. I'm on my way to a birthday party."

He laughed as he tossed the last words at her, and heard her scream of fury as he set off at a canter. "No, goddamn, no. Come back here, you rotten bastard," she cried after him, but he rode away without looking back.

He turned north, into the hills, and rode until the midnight moon hung high. When he halted under a black oak, he stretched out his bedroll and lay down. Agatha Benson's place was on the way to the Wyoming Territory. He frowned as he thought about his bargain with Sherwood Leeds. That old fox had played out his role, knowing it was exactly that, and trusted him to keep his end of it. But a short detour wouldn't be violating the agreement, Fargo told himself and heard his inner oath. A detour to Agatha's would take a day at least, maybe two. Damn Sherwood Leeds, he swore again. The wily old ramrod knew the mark of a man. It was one of his qualities of leadership. Damn him, Fargo swore again as he turned on his side. "Sorry, Agatha. Maybe I can still make it in time. I'll be trying," he murmured softly into the night, and let sleep wrap itself around him.

Morning came in on a warm yellow blanket, and he found a stream for washing and a stand of wild plums for breakfast. He rode at a steady pace the rest of the day, and the peaks of the Medicine Bow Range appeared on his left as dusk fell. He ate some hardtack from his saddlebag and lay down on his bedroll. He had decided not to go into the range but to visit Major Duvall at the stockade below Horse Creek first. Maybe the major would be more cooperative than he'd been with General Leeds. Maybe the troubles were easing off and he could head back to Agatha, Fargo allowed himself to hope as he dropped off to sleep.

He slowed his pace in the morning when Indian signs grew more frequent. His eyes swept the surrounding hills with their thick clusters of black oak, hackberry, hawthorn, and rock outcrops. He came onto part of a gauntlet and halted to examine the markings. "Cheyenne," he grunted after a moment as he studied the rectangles within rectangles, stiffly formal in design.

He rode on with his eyes narrowed. This was Cheyenne country, but the Arapaho could turn up, as could the Teton-Dakota. But now the Pawnee were here, too. They had been moving steadily westward for years and were perhaps the most dangerous of the lot. They were aggressive and smart. One of the four or five tribes that permitted little intermarrying, they were 85 percent pure-blooded. It made for a tightly knit and highly disciplined force.

The sun had passed the noon hour and he rode alongside a low hill when he suddenly heard the whooping cries from the other side of the hill. Unmistakable, they never failed to chill the blood with the pure joy of savage attack curled inside each cry. The rifle shots formed a staccato accompaniment to the wild cries, and Fargo sent the pinto racing up the hillside.

When he reached the top of the hill, he saw a sod-and-stone cabin in a small hollow, a big Owensboro farm wagon loaded with trunks drawn up in front of the cabin. A half-dozen bronze-skinned horsemen were racing around the cabin, pouring arrows and rifle fire into the structure. The return fire came from two figures under the wagon and from inside the cabin.

Fargo drew the big Sharps rifle from its saddle case, put it to his shoulders, and took aim at two of the circling figures, waiting till they came around directly in front of the house. Then he fired, two shots that sounded almost as one. Both Indians flew from their ponies as he sent the Ovaro racing down the hill. He saw the other four red men wheel around and suddenly two more appeared from over another rise to his right. But Fargo was firing as he raced downhill and a third Indian toppled from his short-legged pony with a guttural cry. The Trailsman saw the others turn and start to race off toward the rise as he reached the cabin and leapt from the horse before it came to a halt. He hit the ground on both feet, heels digging into the ground, and dived behind the side of the wagon as a pair of shots slammed into the ground.

He crouched there and brought the rifle up again as the attackers raced across the hillside, firing downward. He ducked two arrows that struck the end of the wagon, too close for comfort, and he slid around to the rear of the wagon. He glimpsed into the open door of the cabin and saw a portly woman with an old single-shot rifle and a still-older woman with gray hair who held a heavy old Colt-Paterson five-shot single-action pistol in one hand.

Fargo brought his eyes back to the hillside as the attackers made another run along the sloping land. He drew his Colt, fired, and saw one of the Indians clutch his shoulder but stay on his pony.

When they reached the end of the hillside, the Indians turned and raced up over the top of the hill, to vanish down the other side.

Fargo pushed to his feet and saw three figures crawl from under the wagon, one a middle-aged man, the other an elderly man, and a young woman with light-brown hair worn long and loose and hazel eyes. She had pronounced cheekbones, a wide mouth, and a short nose—a strong face that just missed being rawboned with its own very defined attractiveness. Tall, clad in a long brown dress that buttoned down the front, she kept hold of her rifle and Fargo saw that her breasts pulled hard at the buttons of the dress.

"Thanks, mister," the middle-aged man said. "I'm Howie Atkins. This is my pa, Ed, and our niece, Clarissa Brown. Your arrival made the difference."

"Glad I was nearby. Name's Fargo . . . Skye Fargo," the Trailsman said, and the young woman stepped forward with a smile.

"That was pretty fancy shooting, Fargo," she said.

"I manage," Fargo said, and glanced at the four inert forms on the ground. "You got one on your own."

"Clarissa," Howie Atkins said. "She's a fine shot."

Fargo stepped close to one of the slain attackers and his gaze held on the Indians moccasins. "Pawnee," he said.

"Of course Pawnee," the older man said. "They've been raiding and killing all over the territory. We were all loaded up to go to the army stockade when they hit us. A lot of farmers and settlers have gone there. They're living in tents, but they're living."

The sudden movement at the top of the hill caught Fargo's ears first, then his eyes as he swiveled and saw two of the Pawnee had suddenly reappeared. They sat their ponies and stared down into the hollow.

"They seem to be looking at you, Fargo," Clarissa observed.

"They are," Fargo said, and felt the frown cross his brow as he stared back at the two distant figures. Suddenly, both Pawnee wheeled their ponies and disappeared down the other side of the hill.

"What was that all about?" Howie Atkins asked.

"Beats me," Fargo said. "Maybe they're making me into a marked man."

Two women came from the house and Howie turned to them. "My wife, Annie, and Grandma Atkins," he introduced. "We're going to go on to the stockade, Fargo. This only made me more certain I'm doing the right thing."

"It's a fair ride. I'll tag along with you," Fargo said.

"We'd be real grateful," the man said, and Fargo helped the old lady into the wagon. The rig held traveling bags, hatboxes, and chairs as well as trunks.

Clarissa went behind the house and reappeared on a nice, light-brown filly with good lines. Some standard-bred blood in it, he decided. As he pulled himself onto the Ovaro, Clarissa swung in beside him and modestly closed a button that had popped open across her breast.

"That's a fine-looking Ovaro you ride, Fargo. The Pawnee won't have trouble remembering that horse," she said.

"Good. Maybe they'll give me a wide berth," Fargo said as he rode alongside the big Owensboro with the young woman. "Anyone know why the Pawnees have gone on such a rampage?" he asked.

"No, but they're sure as hell on the warpath," Howie Atkins answered.

"How long have they been on it?" Fargo asked.

"Well, they'd been doing some raiding for months, the usual Indian attacks, but all hell broke loose a few weeks ago," the man answered, and Fargo grimaced at the reply.

It drew an unusual pattern but not one that proved anything. Maybe the Pawnee had simply decided to escalate their attacks. Maybe they were trying to show the Cheyenne how well they could wage war.

Clarissa's voice broke into his thoughts. "They follow a chief named Red Buffalo," she said, "according to the squaws who come to the stockade to sell things. It's said he's the smartest and most powerful of all the Pawnee chiefs."

"And maybe the most bloodthirsty," Fargo added as he spurred the Ovaro a dozen yards ahead of the wagon. Clarissa Brown caught up to him as he scanned the land ahead with its low rolling hills. The wagon followed the level paths in between as he continued to ride ahead, the young woman beside him. "You come out here with the Atkins?" he asked her.

"From Nebraska," she said.

"No husband?"

"Nope."

He tossed a sidelong glance at her. "Fine, good-looking young woman like you? Doesn't seem right," he said.

"There was a young man. He was supposed to follow me out a few months later. He hasn't shown up yet," Clarissa said with a shade of bitterness in her voice. "It's been over a year."

"You've been waiting all that time?"

"Yes. It becomes a habit after a while. Or maybe a virtue," Clarissa said. "But I didn't figure to be killed by Indians while I was waiting."

Fargo reined to a halt and held up one hand, and she fell silent as he listened. "Hoofbeats," he said, and she picked up the sound.

"More Pawnee?" she asked, alarm instantly in her voice.

"No. These are horses wearing shoes. It's a heavier sound," he said. His eyes were on a stand of black oak when the line of blue-uniformed riders came into view. They rode in a column of twos with an officer in the lead, and he counted ten troopers, the usual patrol complement. The column came to a halt and Fargo saw the young lieutenant execute a brisk salute.

"Lieutenant Baker, B Patrol, Fifth U.S. Cavalry," he said, his eyes moving to the wagon as it rolled up. "You folk on your way to the post?"

"We are," Howie Atkins said.

"You have Indian trouble?" the lieutenant asked.

"You could call it that. We'd likely be dead if Fargo here hadn't come along," Atkins said.

Lieutenant Baker brought his eyes to the big man on the Ovaro. "You passing through?" he asked.

"Fact is I'm on my way to see Major Duvall," Fargo said. "Got a letter from General Leeds."

"You're a courier?" the lieutenant asked.

"Not exactly," Fargo answered, and saw a wary respect come into the lieutenant's young face. He was still gathering thoughts when the six bronze-skinned horsemen appeared atop a ridge to the right.

Surprise flooded the lieutenant's face, almost a moment of panic he instantly put down. Fargo's eyes went to the line of Pawnee atop the ridge.

They were plainly waiting, and he turned as he heard the lieutenant bark orders.

"Company prepare to attack," Lieutenant Baker snapped out crisply.

"Whoa, there. You don't want to do that," Fargo said.

"Orders, mister," the lieutenant said.

"Orders?" Fargo echoed.

"Major Duvall's orders. We're to attack or give chase whenever we see the enemy, at all times," the young officer said.

Fargo's eyes went to the line of Pawnee again. They hadn't moved. "Why, for God's sake?" he snapped at Baker.

"To keep the pressure on the Pawnee, Major Duvall said. To let them know they'll be attacked whenever and wherever we find them," the lieutenant said, and turned to Howie Atkins. "You can continue on to the fort in safety. They'll be too busy with us to bother you."

"Now, hold on, Lieutenant. I think you'd best not go charging after those Pawnee," Fargo cautioned.

"Orders, mister. Orders." Lieutenant Baker drew his saber and barked commands at the patrol. "Charge," he shouted, and the troopers were into a gallop almost instantly as they followed him up the hill. Fargo watched the Pawnee turn and disappear and he swore silently.

"Let's get out of here," Atkins said, and sent the wagon rolling forward. Fargo rode along, his mouth a tight line, and felt Clarissa's eyes on him. He stayed with the wagon for perhaps another five minutes when he reined up sharply.

"You go on," he said. "You'll be safe. The lieutenant was right about that much."

"You're going after him, aren't you?" Clarissa said.

"He's going to need any help he can get," Fargo said as he turned the Ovaro. "I only hope I'm not too late."

"I'm going with you," Clarissa said. "Any help he can get," she said, cutting off his protest.

Fargo shrugged and sent the Ovaro streaking up the hillside. The brown filly stayed close and he searched the terrain on the other side until he picked up the hoofprints. They had chased the Pawnee downhill, deeper into a kind of truncated valley where a tall stand of bur oak blocked his view. They were half-way through the oak when they heard the gunshots, no concentrated cavalry-style fusillades but sporadic defensive fire.

"Damn," Fargo spit out, and spurred the pinto on faster through the trees. He reached the end of the oak and slowed as he took in the scene in front of him. Lieutenant Baker had taken cover behind some rocks and a fallen tree, pinned down, while almost a dozen Pawnee raced back and forth on both sides of him, pouring arrows in clusters into their quarry.

Fargo counted five blue-uniformed figures on the ground and three Pawnee as he reined up at the edge of the trees and leapt to the ground, the big Sharps in one hand, his Colt in the other. Clarissa halted and swung to the ground with her rifle. "Lay down a barrage," he said. "Fire and reload as fast as you can. Bring down any you can, but I want firepower more than accuracy. I want them to think the lieutenant might have reinforcements arriving."

She nodded, stretched out on the ground beside him, and began to fire. He saw one of the racing horsemen fly from his pony and he began to shoot with both hands, laying down a volley with the Sharps and the Colt. Another Pawnee fell to the ground and he saw the others wheel their ponies and race into the trees at the other end of the lay of bottomland. He had reloaded and he sent another volley from both guns into the trees while Clarissa added her own backup fire. He could see the Pawnee inside the distant oaks, gathered together, suddenly turn and race away. He lowered both guns and let a long sigh escape him.

"It worked. They're leaving," Clarissa murmured excitedly.

"They weren't sure what they'd be up against. They weren't going to let themselves be caught in a trap. Pawnee caution, and I counted on it," Fargo said. "We got lucky." He waited, made certain the Pawnee had indeed left before he swung into the saddle and moved down from the trees with Clarissa. He saw Lieutenant Baker's figure rise, the side of his temple trickling blood, his eyes on the two figures that moved toward him.

"Just you two?" the lieutenant breathed in awe.

"That's right. Gather up your casualties," Fargo said.

"We were chasing after them and ran into an ambush," Baker said.

"Planned, and waiting for you and your damn fool orders," Fargo snapped.

The young officer, his face strained, made no reply and turned to what was left of his patrol force. "Place the dead across their saddles. We'll be going back now," he said.

Fargo hung behind with Clarissa as the silent line of uniformed figures, the living sheperding the dead, moved through the oak, out the other side and onto the level land that weaved its way between the hills.

They had ridden some fifteen minutes when two Pawnee appeared on a ridge and stared down at them.

"Shit," Lieutenant Baker hissed. "Prepare for attack."

"Just keep riding," Fargo called, his eyes on the two Pawnee.

"They're staring at you, Fargo, just the way the other two did," Clarissa observed.

"It sure seems that way." Fargo frowned as he moved steadily forward.

The two Pawnee stared down at him for another minute and then vanished into the high trees.

"Why?" Clarissa asked.

"Damned if I know," Fargo said. He saw the lieutenant's expression of relief as the two braves disappeared.

The day was starting to wane when Fargo saw the army post appear, a wooded stockade with a single lookout tower in one corner. No real fort such as Pitt, Cumberland, or Laramie, it nonetheless boasted a barracks and a long stable building. Three clusters of tents were grouped around the side walls, and as the lieutenant led his grim procession through the front gate, a number of troopers rushed forward.

"There's the wagon," Clarissa said, and gestured to where the big Owensboro stood alongside a half-erected tent. "Will you come over later?" she asked.

"I'll try. Thanks for the help back there," he said. "You're not the average young woman."

Clarissa smiled and he realized it was the first time he had seen her do so. Her strong face took on a flash of girlish modesty that made her look younger than she was. "I'm average. I just shoot better than most," she said.

"More guts than most," he corrected, and she rode toward the wagon after tossing another smile at him, her long back swaying gently.

He turned and rode into the stockade, his eyes sweeping the inner yard. He saw the sentries atop the stockade wall walkways and, at the far corner of the post, a thick-walled guardhouse with one barred window. He noticed, with a stab of curiosity, at least a dozen armed troopers standing guard outside. The regimental flag over a doorway marked the post office. He drew to a halt outside, dismounted, and saw Lieutenant Baker emerge with a man wearing the gold leaves of a major on his crisp uniform.

"That's the man, sir," Baker said, spotting Fargo. "He and a young lady saved the rest of us from being slaughtered."

"The patrol owes you a great debt, mister," the major said, and Fargo took in a man of medium height and a trim, erect stance. His face just avoided being hawkish, with a thin, curving nose, piercing brown eyes, thin lips, and a high forehead. "I'm Major Duvall," the officer said. "You told the lieutenant you were on your way to see me?"

"I've a message from General Leeds," Fargo said, and saw Duvall's face tighten at once.

"Come inside," he said, and Fargo followed him into the small office where a large map of the territory hung against one wall dotted with red pins. Fargo handed the major General Leeds' letter and watched the man read it with a tight face. "So the general has sent you here to spy on my operation," the major said when he finished.

"I wouldn't say that," Fargo answered. "He wants to know why you haven't answered any of his communications or sent a report back."

"I've nothing conclusive to report yet," Major Duvall said. "We have a fluid situation here. You're not a military man, so perhaps you don't know what that means."

"To me, it means you've a powerful Pawnee chief on the warpath and you're sending your patrols out with damn-fool orders that'll get them all killed," Fargo said, almost agreeably.

Duvall's face darkened. "You witnessed an unfortunate incident," he snapped.

"I witnessed the result of your orders," Fargo said. "You've been having your patrols chase after every Pawnee they see. It didn't take this Red Buffalo long to see how to turn that to his advantage."

"I may modify that order, but I'll bring down that damn savage very soon," Major Duvall said, and Fargo caught the trace of smugness in his voice. "Then we'll see what the good General Leeds has to say."

"I'm sure he'll be happy to get the good news," Fargo said.

"He'll be green with envy while biting his tongue. He was against my assignment here. He'll have to eat crow," Major Duvall said, a self-satisfied smile coming to his thin lips. He glanced down at the letter again. "You're to assist me in any way you can, it says here," Duvall said. "You'll assist me by staying out of my way, Fargo. Or by leaving."

"Everything in time, Major." Fargo smiled but drew only a hard-eyed stare in response.

"You can find an extra bunk in the barracks," Duvall said, and Fargo smiled at the derogation in the gesture.

"I'll manage," he said, and strode from the office with Duvall following. He paused outside to see that night had settled down over the land. His eyes went to the dozen troopers outside the guardhouse. "You always keep that many men on duty at the guardhouse?" he asked.

"Only when we have especially nasty prisoners," Duvall said, and turned back into his office. Fargo started to lead the Ovaro across the compound when Lieutenant Baker hurried up to him.

"We'd be honored if you'd join us at officer's mess for supper," the lieutenant said.

"My pleasure." Fargo nodded and followed to the officers' quarters, where he was introduced to three equally young lieutenants and a good meal of chili over buffalo. "Things as bad as they seem to me?" Fargo asked as he ate, and he saw the exchange of cautious glances between the others.

"The major has his plans and he's convinced they'll put a stop to things. We've been ordered to keep silent about them," Baker said.

"I wouldn't ask you to go against orders," Fargo said. "But if you decide to have a slip of the tongue, I'll be around."

"We'll remember that," one of the others said, a young man named Fullmer.

"Thanks for the meal," Fargo said when he'd finished.

"Thanks for this afternoon," Baker returned. "And give my thanks to that young lady."

"Clarissa Brown. I will," Fargo said, and left with handshakes all around. He strolled from the compound, the pinto following behind him. Two sentries were at the still-open gate as he went outside and found the big Owensboro beside the tent, now fully erected. But like most of the other tents, it was dark and silent, everyone already asleep. He moved slowly past, his thoughts on Major Duvall.

The man seethed with his own goals. Maybe he was afraid of failure. Maybe he wanted personal vengeance. Either could be tied in with the determination to make a name for himself, to prove himself to the world. Whatever his reasons, he wasn't about to be cooperative. And from what he had seen so far, Fargo mused, and the implied remarks of the junior officers, the major's interest was to escalate the conflict, not tone it down. He was a man certain of his goal and without the experience or wisdom to reach it. Always a dangerous mixture, Fargo grimaced.

A voice broke into his thoughts and he halted. "Fargo," it called, and he turned to see Clarissa come from the tent, her tall figure moving with a gentle swaying motion, a shawl around her shoulders and a cotton nightgown beneath. "Been waiting for you to come by," she said. "I couldn't sleep."

"Too much excitement today?" he asked as he halted against the outside of the stockade wall.

"No. I worried, about my sister, Ada," she said, and his frown questioned. "She's on her way out here to be with me. She got a ride on a wagon train that was due to arrive last week. It still hasn't come."

"A week doesn't mean that much," he told her.

"No, but with everything that's been going on, I'm really worried," Clarissa said, and leaned her head against the stockade wall. The shawl parted and the soft swell of her breasts rose up over the edge of the square neckline of the nightgown. The moonlight on the planes of her face gave her a soft beauty that had a kind of unearthly loveliness. "The Atkins are family, distant cousins and good people, but sometimes I feel very alone. This is one of those nights," she said.

"I'm going to bed down over in those trees," Fargo said, gesturing to a line of cottonwoods a few hundred yards from the post. "You're welcome to come along."

She turned a quizzical smile his way. "Meaning what, exactly?"

"Meaning maybe you won't feel so alone," he said.

"Nothing else?" She smiled.

"Not unless you want something else."

"No, I just want not to feel so alone," she said. "I'll get my blanket."

He nodded and watched her move silently back to the tent. The two sentries closed the stockade gate and Fargo looked up to see the head of a sentry atop the walkway inside the compound.

The silence of sleep and the night descended fully when Clarissa hurried back, the blanket folded over one arm. The night was warm, but the blanket would soften the ground. He started to walk toward the cottonwoods with her, the Ovaro following, when he heard the pounding of hooves at a full gallop. He dived to the ground, yanking Clarissa with him, rolled with her, and turned to lie half-across her, the big Colt in his hand.

The sentries atop the stockade were aware of the hoofbeats now and he heard their shouts of alarm as two near-naked riders raced out of the darkness, one holding a lance. The sentries began to fire, but the Indians lay low across their ponies as they raced to within a hundred feet of the stockade. He held fire, his finger poised on the trigger of the Colt, as he saw the one rider throw the lance into the ground. Then both wheeled off in opposite directions and raced away. Shouts and cries of fright came from the tents and inside the stockade as the shots woke everyone, and Fargo rose and pulled Clarissa to her feet.

She went with him as he walked toward the lance that quivered in the ground, and the compound gates swung open. He saw Major Duvall, still struggling into his uniform jacket, rush out with a half-dozen troopers.

Fargo reached the lance with Clarissa just as the major did and he saw the thin square of deerskin wrapped around the center of the lance. It had come loose at one end and Major Duvall pulled the rest of it free and stared down at it, a frown digging itself into his brow. He looked up and handed the square of deerskin to Fargo.

"What the hell do you make of this?" Duvall asked, and Fargo looked at the drawing of a horse that took up most of the square. "A drawing of a horse. What the hell does that mean?" the major barked.

Fargo stared at the drawing, the outlines of the horse filled in with black along the forequarters and the hindquarters. "It's a drawing of my horse, my Ovaro," he said softly.

4

Major Duvall pulled the square of deerskin around so he could look at it again. "By God, it just might be," he muttered. "But what the hell does it mean?"

"It's a message. I'd say it means Red Buffalo wants to talk to me," Fargo offered.

"What the hell does he want to talk to you for, Fargo? You know this damn savage?" the major barked.

"No."

"Then the hell with his message."

"He must have his reasons. Aren't you curious?"

"No. Forget it," Duvall snapped.

"Sorry, I'm not doing that," Fargo said, and the major's eyes narrowed at him.

"You going to answer this damn message?" Duvall asked.

"Come morning," Fargo said.

"And I'm saying forget it. This savage is the enemy and I'm ordering you not to communicate with the enemy," the major said.

"You can't do that," Fargo returned. "First, I'm not in your army, and second, I already have my orders from General Sherwood. They are to do whatever I can to cool things. I'm going to hear what Red Buffalo wants to say."

"It's probably a trick to get hold of you for helping my patrol. You're being a damn fool," the major said.

"My decision, my neck," Fargo said, and Duvall turned his back to him and strode into the compound.

The troopers pulled the gate closed and Fargo felt Clarissa's hand on his arm. He turned and walked into the trees with her, took his saddlebag down as she spread her blanket alongside.

"Maybe the major is right, Fargo," she said softly.

"No, there's more to it than that. Damned if I've the faintest notion what, though." He shed clothes, down to his drawers, and stretched out on the bedroll, aware of Clarissa's eyes moving up and down the symmetry of his smoothly muscled body. He felt her hand move, curl around his.

"Good night, Fargo," she said, and he listened to her fall asleep, her hand tightly around his. She had her own quiet strengths, her own containments, and he kept her hand in his as he let sleep come to him.

When night finally eased itself into morning, her hand was still in his. He felt her stir as he rose and slipped from her grip. He used his canteen to wash and he was almost dressed when she woke and rubbed sleep from her eyes.

The neckline of her nightgown dipped to one side, to reveal the soft curve of one creamy-white breast. She rose as Fargo strapped on his gun belt. There was none of the tousled, sleepy-eyed look to her that was with most women when they woke, he noticed. She was clear-eyed and poised as she pushed to her feet and came to him.

"How will you find him?" she asked.

"I won't. His scouts will find me. They'll be watching," he told her.

She leaned forward and held her lips against his for a brief moment, a soft, tender touch. "Be careful," she murmured. "Come back."

"I plan to," he said, put his gear together, and climbed onto the Ovaro. She was still in the trees, watching him go as he rode off into the new sun.

He headed north, through the hill country, and he guessed he'd traveled for almost an hour when he saw the half-naked horsemen, lance in hand, looking down at him from a rock. He slowed and another bronzed-skinned rider appeared to his right, then a third to his left. He turned the Ovaro toward them and they moved closer together and began to ride northward ahead of him, a silent escort.

He followed them upward as they moved into the hills, through narrow rock-bound passages and across open flatland patches. He spotted other Pawnee warriors watching from high crevices as he made mental notes of bent trees, twisted passages, rock formations, and any landmark that seemed worth cataloging. He found himself moving through a dense thicket of black oak and suddenly the camp spread out before him in a long, cleared area.

The three braves he had followed dropped back to surround him as they rode into camp. The Pawnee spoke the Caddoan tongue, as did the Wichita. Fargo was most fluent in the Siouan, but there were many words in the Caddoan that were very similar to the Siouan, which was spoken by most of the great tribal families. Because the Pawnee had continued to push westward, they had drawn more and more of the Sioux language into their own. Together with his knowledge of sign language, he didn't expect to have trouble communicating with the Pawnee chief.

As Fargo rode deeper into the camp, he saw it was no trail camp but the full-scale, permanent camp with squaws and naked kids and old women tending to hide-beating chores. He saw an extra amount of braves, close to a hundred, who watched him enter with faces like stone carvings. A long row of tepees lined one side of the camp with a thatched-roof council house made of branches at one end. A deep-running stream flowed along behind the line of tepees. As he moved his eyes slowly back across the camp to the other end, he felt the stab in the pit of his stomach as he saw two Conestoga wagons pulled behind a large tepee decorated with drawings of hunting and war.

The three braves halted in front of the tepee and Fargo dismounted, his eyes on the open tent flap. The figure that slowly emerged was tall, clothed in leggins and a buckskin breechclout dyed deep blue, a beaded armband worn just over the biceps and a lone eagle's feather. Braided black hair glistened with fish oil in the sun.

Fargo took in a massive man, a large nose and heavy lips, and a big jaw, a head that was indeed reminiscent of a buffalo's powerful form. He had a torso to match, with powerful shoulders and arms.

"So this is Fargo, the great tracker and warrior," the Indian said.

"How do you come to know me?" Fargo asked.

"A man leaves his shadow behind him. Words are like seeds carried by the wind. They scatter far," the Pawnee said. "You killed the Sioux Chief Mountain Lion. You fought the Cheyenne Chief Thunderhawk and you slew the great Nez Percé Chief Strong Elk. There were others. Word of your deeds have traveled far. Pictures have been drawn of you and your great war horse."

"Your braves attacking the cabin remembered those pictures," Fargo said, and the Pawnee nodded. "But Red Buffalo did not send for me to talk about coups and great deeds."

The Pawnee chief's heavy face shifted itself into a

half-smile. "No. You are here to listen, and then to obey," he said.

"I obey only myself," Fargo spoke up. Fear or weakness would be a mistake, he knew. Better to anger the Pawnee than to show anything else.

The Pawnee took in Fargo's words and he saw the Indian's eyes narrow, but he made no direct reply.

"This blue-coat chief, we will speak first of him," Red Buffalo said.

"He is called major," Fargo said. "Major Duvall."

"He has not listened to me," the Pawnee chief said. "I have sent messages for him with the half-breed squaws who trade at his camp. So I have spoken with my warriors, with the killing and raiding, and he still does not listen."

"What messages have you sent him?" Fargo asked.

"I have told him to release my daughter, Moonglow," the Indian said, his voice growing suddenly thunderous.

Fargo felt the shock of surprise spiral through him. "The major has your daughter?" He frowned.

"One of his band of bluecoats came upon her. They were lucky and they took her," Red Buffalo said.

"How long ago?" Fargo asked.

"After the moon was round," the Indian said.

Fargo let thoughts race. Less than a month, but a few weeks at least. Suddenly all the extra patrols in front of the guardhouse took on new meaning. Holding the Pawnee chief's daughter had set the tribe on the warpath, a bloodbath of savage attacks. Fargo found himself anxious to hear Duvall's reasoning, but he decided to quickly make something clear to the Pawnee. "I do not command the major," he said.

"I know only one blue-coat can command another," Red Buffalo said with a trace of impatience.

"Then why have you asked me here?" Fargo persisted.

"I know this blue-coat's plans as if I were inside his body," the chief said, lifting his massive head high. "He wants me to attack to free my daughter. He knows I must do this. He will try to make me attack at his time and his place. He knows I will lose many, many warriors in such an attack, perhaps all my fine young braves, and that is what he wants. Even if I take back Moonglow, it will be at the cost of most of my braves. A Chief without warriors is like a cougar without teeth or claws. He has no weapons with which to fight. He is without strength."

"But he would lose many, too," Fargo said.

"He plans to win, to survive even with his losses and then call in more soldiers in weeks. But great warriors are not made in weeks but in the passing of many, many moons. They must grow from boyhood into manhood," the chief said.

"You still do not tell me why you sent for me," Fargo said.

"Because I am not going to do what this blue-coated chief wants. I am not going to lose all my fine warriors," the Pawnee said. "You are going to free my daughter."

Fargo blinked as the words bounced inside him, each bounce a resounding thud. At another time and with another man he might have wondered if he had heard correctly. But here, in front of the Pawnee chief, he knew he had heard all too well. "Has the great Pawnee chief been drinking firewater?" he asked. "Why does he think I could do such a thing?"

"One man who can move as he wishes, one man

who can come close, can free Moonglow," the Indian said. "One who has proved many times that he is a great warrior. Such a one is you."

Fargo swore silently at the wily truth in the Pawnee's thinking. "I asked why does Red Buffalo think I could do such a thing. Why does he think I would do this?"

"Come with me," the Indian said, and Fargo followed the massive figure as he marched toward the two Conestoga wagons. Red Buffalo passed both and halted at the other side of the wagons, where Fargo saw the figures tied to the trees with lengths of rawhide thongs. He cursed in bitter silence as his eyes moved along the line of men, women, and children, the members of the two Conestogas. A mixture of fear, surprise, and uncertain hope filled each pair of eyes, even the smallest of the children. He stepped forward, swept the captives with a long glance.

"I'll help you, I promise. Somehow, I'll find a way," he said, and his glance paused on a young girl, not quite as tall as Clarissa but with the same strong planes in her face. "Are you Ada Brown?" he asked. She tried to answer, but only small sobbing sounds came from her and she settled for a vigorous nod. Fargo turned away to meet the Pawnee chief's black-coal eyes.

"This is why you will do what I say," Red Buffalo intoned. "If you do not, I will kill one of these prisoners every day and leave the body for the soldiers to find. Man, woman, child. One a day."

He stopped speaking and Fargo wrestled with the whirlwind of thoughts that spun through his mind. The Pawnee made no idle threat. That was the first fact above all others. He was as cunning as he was ruthless. He had orchestrated a plan that used every facet of human behavior, harsh reality, practical wisdom, conscience and duty, existence and morals. Of course he brought no profound analysis to his actions but they sprang from an instinctual command of human behavior that outmatched anything learned from books.

The Pawnee chief waited, a hint of triumph touching the massive head. Not yet, Fargo muttered to himself. Not yet, you cunning bastard. He grimaced as he clung to one thought that rose from the whirlwind. He needed time, time to meet with Duvall, time to find a way out, time to save two wagonloads of innocent people.

"No," he said firmly and saw the surprise leap into Red Buffalo's face, quickly joined by an angry frown. "Not yet," added quickly. "I want to talk to the major."

"He will not listen to you," the Indian said.

"I have ways to make him listen," Fargo tossed back, aware that the Pawnee couldn't completely dismiss the possibility. "I want three days," Fargo said. "Three days and I will come back."

Chief Red Buffalo considered for another pause and finally nodded. "Three moons," he said, and Fargo held back his sigh of relief.

The Pawnee hadn't agreed out of trust or compassion, Fargo realized, but only because he had nothing to lose by waiting another three days.

Fargo followed the big form back to the tepee. He pulled himself onto the Ovaro and Red Buffalo retired into his tepee without a backward glance, the gesture one of dismissal and arrogant confidence. Three braves accompanied him all the way back to the low hills before they peeled off and rode away in separate directions

Fargo rode slowly and let his thoughts settle down into something other than a whirling jumble. He still stood in awe of the bold genius of Red

Buffalo's ultimatum, but he pushed awe aside and let anger spiral as he brought his thoughts to Major Duvall. He couldn't tell Duvall the real reason Red Buffalo had summoned him. The Indian's ultimatum was one he might yet have to face, a decision he might still have to make, and it would have to be a lone decision. But he refused to dwell on that. Instead, he concentrated his thoughts on Duvall. He'd tell the major that Red Buffalo had summoned him to transmit the ultimatum on the prisoners of the wagon train. He'd make Duvall see that there really was no choice but to give in to the Pawnee.

Fargo saw the shadows of dusk sliding across the land as he came in sight of the stockade. He rode past the tents quickly, eager to avoid meeting Clarissa until he'd faced Duvall. He dismounted inside the stockade and hurried to Duvall's office. A trooper admitted him and Duvall rose from behind his desk, his piercingly hard eyes probing.

"You're back alive," the major commented. "I wondered if you would be. You meet with that damn savage?"

"I did," Fargo said. "Why didn't you tell me you were holding his daughter?"

"Didn't see it as any of your concern," Duvall said.

Fargo felt his temper flare. "General Leeds sent me to find out about things here and you say that's none of my concern?" he thrust. "That's a pretty weak excuse."

"I have the situation well in hand," the major said loftily.

"You've a damn tiger by the tail, that's what you have," Fargo shot back. "Turn the girl loose."

Duvall stared at him. "You crazy, mister?" he

barked. "She's the key to everything. I'm going to use her to destroy that stinking savage."

"She's the key, you're right there. He's got a wagon train of hostages. You let his daughter go and he'll release the hostages. Otherwise, he's going to kill one each day and drop the body on your doorstep."

"So that's why he sent for you, so you could bargain for him," Duvall said, a sneer in his voice.

"He sent for me so you couldn't say he was bluffing. He wanted me to see the hostages with my own eyes," Fargo returned, more certain than ever that he could tell the major nothing else.

"All right, you've seen them. It doesn't change anything," Duvall said.

"You can't do this. You can't sacrifice the lives of more innocent people than you have already."

"I'm saving future lives by putting an end to that damn savage."

"The price is too high for that kind of hope," Fargo said. "You've got to let the girl go."

Duvall slammed his fist down on the desk. "Like hell. She's my prisoner and she's going to stay that. Do you hear me, Fargo? I know just what I'm doing."

Fargo swore inwardly and decided on another approach to the man. "It's not going to look good for you when I tell General Leeds you sacrificed the lives of all those men and women, and children for one Indian girl," he said.

Duvall returned an icy smile filled with smug certainty. "It's going to look real good on my record when I wipe out that Pawnee. That's what people will remember, and that's what I'm going to do."

"What if he all but wipes you out? You'll lose

most of your own men no matter what," Fargo said.

"They're soldiers. They're in this man's army to put their lives on the line," Duvall snapped coldly.

"Not for a damn-fool, unnecessary reason."

Duvall leaned forward. "The Indian won't wipe me out. He's got to try to save his daughter, and he knows I'll destroy him when he does. That's why he's using you. He's desperate."

Fargo almost smiled at the ironic truth in the man's words. Red Buffalo was desperate, but the major's savage cared more about his warriors than the fancy-schooled officer. And to add even greater irony, he played on the civilized concepts of morality and compassion for the innocent. He was using the white man's most precious tenets to his own advantage. "Savage" was perhaps only a word, he thought as he returned the major's cold stare. "Let the girl go," he said.

"Go to hell," Duvall roared. "I told you to stay out of my way, Fargo. Instead, you're running interference for a damn Pawnee."

"I'm running interference for the innocent people of that wagon train and all the troopers you're going to needlessly sacrifice," Fargo flung back.

"What else do you figure to do to get in my way, Fargo?"

"I haven't decided yet," Fargo snapped, and he saw the man's eyes grow smaller. It had not been a wise answer, he realized, but his fury had ruled. He turned and strode from the office and felt Duvall's eyes boring into his back as though they were knife marks. The man was obsessed, beyond reasoning with, beyond caring about human life. He panted for glory, for a spectacular victory and he was willing to sacrifice anything and anyone to get it.

Fargo went into the darkness outside and led the

Ovaro from outside the office. He paused as he saw the heavy patrols outside the guardhouse and sauntered over. As he drew closer, the troopers stopped their pacing and brought their rifles up and he saw the figure come toward him. The young face frowned as he halted.

"Fargo," Lieutenant Baker said in surprise. "Sorry, you can't come any closer. I drew officer of the night duty tonight."

"It's all right, Lieutenant," Fargo said. "I know who's in your guardhouse." He smiled at the surprise that flooded the officer's face and his eyes went past Baker. There was but one small, barred window in the guardhouse, he noted, a narrow door at the front of the thick-walled structure. Even without the guards outside, it would be a difficult place to break into, he decided. "Good night, Lieutenant." He smiled and led the pinto across the compound.

He walked slowly, not ready to face the enormity of it all. He pushed aside the dilemma that tried to rise up in front of him like some monstrous apparition, replete with mocking laugh. He cursed Duvall's obsessive ruthlessness and Red Buffalo's consummate cunning. Then he remembered the hollowed eyes of the captives and cursed again. He'd try Duvall again in the morning. Perhaps a night's sleep would give the man a different perspective, he told himself, even though he knew how slim the chances were of that happening. Yet he would try again. He could do no less.

When he left the compound and passed along the tents, he saw a figure sitting outside the tent beside the Owensboro.

Clarissa rose as he approached and hurried to him. "I saw you go into the compound," she said. "I've been waiting since."

72

"Duvall took more time than I expected," he said.

She studied his face. "You're not happy."

"Not especially," he admitted. "I'm going to bed down."

"I'll come."

"You want to get your blanket?"

"No," she said, and fell in step beside him.

He went into the trees again, stayed silent until he'd stretched out his bedroll.

"I spent the day being afraid for you," she said. "You saw Red Buffalo, I assume."

"Yes. I saw your sister, too," he said, and watched Clarissa's mouth fall open. Surprise instantly gave way to alarm. "He has the wagon train, everybody that was a part of it," Fargo said, and he told her everything he had told Duvall and then of his talk with the major.

"My God, my God, he can't do that," she muttered. "He just can't turn his back on all those people."

"He can, and he will," Fargo said. "But I'm going to talk to him again tomorrow."

"What if he still refuses?" Clarissa asked. "Is there anything anybody can do?"

"Let's wait and see. One thing at a time," Fargo told her, and she stretched out beside him, her hand stealing into his, her shoulder resting against his arm.

"You're a good man, Fargo," she murmured. "Not just for all you've done, but for letting me stay here with you like this."

"This is the hardest part, honey" he said. "It puts a terrible strain on my good behavior."

She turned, her hazel eyes grave as she looked at him. "I'm sorry," she said.

"How sorry?"

"Not that sorry. Not yet," she answered. "Do you want me to go?"

"Get some sleep," he grunted, and she lay back but her hand stayed in his.

He drew sleep around himself as a protective shawl, shutting out all the things he knew would still be there, come morning. Clarissa slept restlessly, turning and tossing, but never letting go of his hand. He grew quickly used to the rustling sound of her nightdress as she turned, and it was a dim recognition in his brain as he clung to sleep. The night had grown deep when he dimly heard her again, turning restlessly.

But his eyes snapped open. The sound held a difference, soft and rustling but not the same. He started to turn and reach for the Colt at his side when he saw the shadow of the blow come down on him. He managed to half-turn his head and the blow slammed into his temple. He felt a sharp pain as the Colt skittered from his hand into the thick brush. He tried to roll, and took another sledgehammerlike blow just below his neck, and heard Clarissa's half-scream as she woke.

He fell forward, tried to turn, and managed to glimpse a big, bulky figure come down on him again with both fists raised. But suddenly the figure staggered sideways and let out a grunt of pain and he saw Clarissa atop the man's back, one hand yanking at his hair.

The man whirled, bent low, and Clarissa slid from his back. With a massive backhand blow, he smashed his arm into her stomach and she flew in a short arc, to crash into the ground. But the moment had let Fargo regain his feet and he faced the man who came at him again. He saw a square, beefy face with little eyes and close-cropped hair, a powerful torso with big shoulders and arms to match.

The man wore a gray undershirt and brown denim trousers, and Fargo avoided his bull-like charge and sank a left into the man's ribs. His assailant grunted, whirled, and came in with both fists swinging furiously. Fargo gave ground before the collection of hooks, jabs, straight-arm punches, and roundhouse swings. He took most of the blows on his arms and felt their power. When the man slowed to catch his breath, Fargo drove a short, head-snapping left jab to his chin.

His assailant paused, shook away the blow, and received a short right follow-up uppercut. The man staggered back a pace this time and Fargo swung a looping left. But he had hurried the blow and the man pulled backward as the blow grazed his chin. He dived forward, bent low, barreled into Fargo's legs and the Trailsman felt himself go down on his back. Two powerful, thick-fingered hands closed around his throat, instantly closing off air. "Son of a bitch," the man growled as he pressed harder.

Fargo tried to turn and twist and throw him off, but the man was too heavy and kept his straddling position. Fargo felt his breath quickly becoming no more than a thin, rasping sound, and knew that as his breath failed so would his strength. He dug his right heel into the ground and, with his fast-fading strength, brought his leg up as hard as he could. His knees slammed into the man's buttocks and the figure fell forward, not very far but just far enough for him to lose his balance. Fargo twisted hips, used the last of his strength to push arms into the ground, and the man fell to one side, the thick-fingered hands losing their grip on his throat.

The Trailsman rolled away, avoiding a grabbing blow, and leapt to his feet as he gulped in deep breaths. The man was up and coming at him again but Fargo felt wind and strength flowing back into his body. He lashed out with two quick jabs, which the man brushed aside, came forward, and took a jolting right cross on the point of the chin. He halted, staggered, and Fargo's left hook sent him spinning into the fall. He hit the ground and Fargo leapt after him, started to reach down to twist his beefy face around. The man whirled and Fargo caught the glint of moonlight on a knife blade as it slashed sideways at him.

The tip of the blade grazed his muscled abdomen as he managed to pull back, and he retreated as his assailant regained his feet and came at him again, the knife held forward not unlike a short lance. The man poked the blade at him, a thick hunting knife, Fargo saw as he circled back. The man poked again, to the right, then the left, in the center, and then on both sides, a snarling smile edging his beefy face.

Fargo continued to circle backward, leg muscles tensed, his eyes on every quick, forward feint of the blade. He was ready when the man stopped feinting and lunged forward with the knife. Fargo twisted away, ducked, and brought a looping left up from a half-crouch.

The blow caught his opponent alongside the jaw and the man staggered sideways but managed to whirl and slash out with the knife as Fargo came forward. The Trailsman ducked under the blow and the man's feet left the ground as he leapt with another slashing blow. Fargo stayed ducked low, a half-crouch, and felt the blow whistle over his back. He drove his shoulder into the man's belly and heard the grunt of pain that followed. He straightened up as the man staggered back, his mouth still open as he gasped for breath. Fargo started a looping right and drew the blow back as he saw the man raise the knife. He measured seconds as the knife came down at him, then he shot his hand out and closed it around the wrist of the man's knife hand.

He twisted, pulled the man's arm down along with its own descending momentum, and felt the knife slice into the man's abdomen and down through his belly. Fargo released his grip and watched the figure fall forward, onto his knees, one hand still around the hilt of the knife deep into his groin. A river of red poured from the man and he lifted his beefy face, disbelief in the small eyes and then pitched forward. He lay facedown, groaning sounds coming from him until, with a shudder, he was still.

Fargo looked across to where Clarissa was just pushing herself to a sitting position. She met his eyes and got to her feet and hurried over to him. "Thanks," he said. "It might've been all over at the beginning if it hadn't been for you."

She leaned against him and her eyes went to the inert figure a few yards away. "Who is he? Why did he attack you? Where did he come from?" she murmured.

"Good questions," Fargo said. He stepped from her and knelt down beside the still form. He turned the man onto his back and took in his clothes again, then examined his boots. Everything was determinedly ordinary; he examined the man's hands for rings and found nothing. He began to go through his pockets, taking care to avoid the red stain that soaked the figure from the waist down. But the man's pants pockets held only a few coins. Fargo was about to straighten up when he remembered the man's shirt pocket. He reached inside it, felt something crinkle at his touch, and pulled out a small, rectangular, folded piece of paper. Clarissa came to stand beside him as he unfolded the paper and felt his lips tighten.

"A receipt voucher for a month's pay, issued by the United States Army," Fargo grunted.

"He's a soldier?" Clarissa gasped

"Was a soldier," Fargo corrected. "He made sure there was nothing on him to identify him as that. He just forgot to take this out of his pocket."

"But why? What does it mean?" Clarissa frowned.

"It means I don't have to bother trying to get the major to change his mind tomorrow."

Shock flooded her face. "You saying Major Duvall sent him to kill you?"

"Can't prove it, but I'd bet on it. He decided to make sure I wouldn't be getting in his way," Fargo said, and led Clarissa away. He picked up the bedroll and moved deeper into the trees.

"What are you going to do?" she asked.

"Get in his way," Fargo said, and lay down on the bedroll. She lay down beside him, close against him, and her hand rested on his chest. He had comforted her by being there when she wanted not to be alone and now she was strangely comforting beside him. He didn't want to be alone either. He knew that from the new day forward he would be alone, very alone, and he closed his eyes and wrapped sleep around him. He'd face the decisions he had to make come morning.

He'd have to make his plans then, too, distasteful as they were. He'd have to make them carefully, so very, very carefully.

5

Fargo woke first in the warm morning; he washed and dressed but there was no washing away the grimness that clung to him. When Clarissa woke, looking clear-eyed at once, she rose and he led the Ovaro down from the trees as she walked beside him. He skirted the place where the attack had taken place, and she spoke only when he neared the tent.

"Will I see you tonight?" she asked.

He had one more day to return to the Pawnee chief. "Yes," he said. "But not till tonight."

She nodded in understanding and disappeared inside the tent as he walked on to the stockade.

Troopers were holding a cavalry drill outside, two soldiers manned the walkways and the extra sentries paced back and forth in front of the guardhouse. He saw Duvall in front of his office with one of the young lieutenants, the man named Fuller. " 'Morning," Fargo said. "You missing one of your men?" He tossed out the question casually and caught the moment's tightness that touched Duvall's lips.

"Why? Not that it's any of your business. You're a civilian, mister," the major said.

"Sergeant Brady said that Gilley didn't answer roll call. He hasn't been seen in camp, either," the lieutenant said.

Duvall's glance at the lieutenant was controlled fury. "Thank you, Fullmer," he said.

"Gilley? Beefy-faced man with a close-cropped haircut, army style? Little eyes?" Fargo put in.

"That's him," the lieutenant said.

"You'll find him in the cottonwoods east of the compound. Very dead," Fargo said. "He attacked me last night, tried to kill me. I've a witness."

"My God," Fullmer said.

"Take four men and bring him back," Duvall ordered, and turned to Fargo. "My apologies for the behavior of a United States cavalry soldier. Gilley, unfortunately, was always a troublemaker. Whenever he got drunk, he seemed to go berserk. He'd obviously been drinking heavily."

"I couldn't say. He'd no breath left to smell when it ended," Fargo said. "He made a mistake. Or somebody did," he added offhandedly, and strolled away. He climbed onto the Ovaro as he left the stockade, and rode slowly past the tents where he saw Clarissa with a washbucket of clothes. He rode west as the lieutenant and four soldiers marched toward the cottonwoods; he climbed the side of a low hill, rode along the top, and found a place to halt on a high, moss-covered ledge of rock and earth.

He sat down against the fissured, gray-brown bark of a big box elder, closed his eyes, and heard a long, grim sigh come from deep inside him. He had to make a decision, he'd told himself. But that was untrue. He was making no decision and perhaps that was the part that cut at him the deepest. The Pawnee chief was really pulling the strings, and Fargo grimaced at the thought. He didn't like being a pawn, manipulated by a cunning Indian actually as ruthless as Major Duvall. But the line of captives in the Pawnee camp rose up in front of him again and he knew he was like an actor cast into a role against his will with no choice but to play it out.

He would be walking a deadly path. Duvall wanted nothing better than to find a legitimate excuse to have him shot. Red Buffalo would kill him instantly if he thought he was being tricked. The deadly path grew narrower each time he thought about it. He wrenched his thoughts away from questions of right and wrong, of choices that were really not choices at all. It was time to fill his mind with plans, practical realities of calculations, possibilities, probabilities, all the building blocks for action that would leave no room for searching the soul. He began with the guardhouse and the extra patrols out in front, laid out approaches, discarded most, and finally wound up with three possibly workable alternatives.

The careful planning took up most of the day, and when dusk began to slide its purple fingers across the land, he rose and pulled himself onto the Ovaro. He was tired, mentally fatigued, and he rode back knowing he had formed plans that were, at best, tenuous blueprints.

Night had fallen when he reached the stockade and he dismounted and sauntered inside. He went to the stables and borrowed some oats for the Ovaro, then leisurely led the horse to the water trough and let him drink, all the while studying the guardhouse from different angles. None offered any encouragement and he decided he'd have to try the roof. But he'd have to find the right moment, and that could take time. Morning would bring the third day. He'd have to return to the Pawnee chief. That had been the promise, and if he broke it, the hostages would pay the price.

He finally strolled from the stockade just as the sentries were closing the gate and he saw Clarissa waiting outside the tent. She wore the shawl around her shoulders, the cotton nightgown beneath, and she stepped forward to meet him. She fell in step beside him in silence as he walked west, away from the cottonwoods and up onto a hillock with a dense cover of hawthorn. He found a spot where the moonlight managed to filter through the leaves and set out his bedroll.

"Talk to me, Fargo. Tell me what's going to happen," Clarissa said finally.

"I'm not in the fortune-telling business anymore. Never was much good at it," Fargo said.

"No, you're not one to tell fortunes, but you're one to make things happen. That's a kind of fortune-telling."

His laugh held a wry bitterness. "It's a kind of hoping."

"What are you hoping for, Fargo?"

"I'm hoping I can free your sister and the others," he told her.

She offered a half-smile of resignation. "There's no way if the major won't cooperate. You can't go into the Pawnee camp and take them out."

He swore to himself. He wanted to tell her more, admit how Red Buffalo was using him as puppet. But he didn't dare, not even to her. She'd not be able to hide hope, and hope could make others ask questions. She'd not answer, he was certain; but they'd wonder, and wondering could lead to gossip and perhaps to Duvall's ears.

"There's a way, a slim chance," he said. "I'll not say more."

"I'll not ask more." She nodded and he settled himself on the bedroll. She dropped to her knees beside him. "I've been unfair," Clarissa said, and his glance questioned. "Putting a strain on your good behavior," she finished, and let the shawl fall from her shoulders. Her hand went to a tiny bow at the square neck of the nightgown, pulled on one string, and it came open. The neckline of the gown fell forward loosely, and the soft, twin mounds pushed outwards instantly. She wriggled her shoulder and the garment fell away entirely, sliding down to her knees.

Fargo took in broad, strong shoulders, breasts that were deep and beautifully cupped, curving to large, pink areolae surrounding large but flat pink tips. Beneath them, a rounded rib cage moved into a flat abdomen and, below it, a belly with just a hint of a sensuous curve to it. He saw wide hips, strong, firmly fleshed thighs, and a triangle not very black and not very thick. She stood up, kicked the nightgown away, and let him take in her statuesque beauty.

He reached up and pulled her down to him with one hand as he started to pull off clothes with the other. Her strong-planed face was grave, the hazel eyes staring with directness at him, her full lips slightly parted. He saw her gaze flick to his hard-muscled body as he shed the last of his clothes. He brought his mouth to hers, parted her lips, waited, slowly let his tongue dance against hers, and felt her shudder. Her lips parted, moved, returned his touch, opening, and he probed into the sweetness of her kiss. Her breath drew in, a soft half-gasp that became a quick cry as his hand cupped around one firm breast.

"Oh, oh, God," Clarissa breathed, and he felt her stiffen, shrink back, then come forward as he moved his thumb slowly across the flat pink tip, which grew under his touch. He pulled his lips from hers, brought them down to her breast, and enclosed the sweet nipple in his touch; he sucked gently on it and Clarissa began a long, moaning sound. Her hands closed around the back of his neck and held him against her. "Aaaaah . . .

aaaaaaah," she moaned, her voice deepening, rising, deepening again. He brought one leg up and rested it across her thighs, and the moaning sounds became sharper, quicker. He rubbed his leg against hers and her hips twisted, turned, fell back again. His hands were exploring her long, strong body, touching places not touched before, caressing, inflaming.

Clarissa's soft sounds suddenly stopped and he felt her stiffen as his hand moved through the light triangle and pressed gently on the pubic mound; he lifted his face to glance at her. She lay with her lips parted, her eyes staring, almost as if in suspended animation, frozen in time. He moved his hand down past the thin, wiry bush, kneaded his way through thighs held firmly closed, and touched the dark, warm portal, moistness flowing over him as he found the edge of a liquidlike lip. He pressed gently and moved along its satin smoothness.

Suddenly Clarissa screamed, a short, sharp sound, and her thighs fell open, her strong, young body twisted and came over his, and she rubbed herself up and down his smoothly muscled frame. "Oh, God, oh, God, oh, God," Clarissa half-screamed and seemed suddenly possessed, set aflame with uncontrolled wanting. Her thighs pressed against his sides and she pushed her breasts into his face as she cried out. He stayed against the warm-flowing of her and his own throbbing erectness came against her inner thighs. She screamed at the touch.

She fell onto her back, thighs parted and her hands digging into his shoulders. "Oh, God, yes, yes please, Fargo . . . oh, yes, oh, please," she said, words falling one upon the other in a long breathy cascade of sound. The words turned into a cry as he came forward on her. slid into the warm tunnel slowly, and felt the constricting tightness of her part. The cry became a scream and her heard protest and wanting mixed together in it, pain and pleasure, and then, with overwhelming desire, she pushed forward, her strong back arching and her pelvis striking against his. "Yes, yes, yes, yes, yes," she screamed, and her hazel eyes were suddenly dark, her mouth opening, making sucking motions until he put his lips on hers.

A wild strength was in her, pushing and arching and crying out even as her mouth clung to his, her deep-cupped breasts flattened against his chest. He felt her tiny squeezing around him first, contractions that quickly grew, and she tore her lips from his as her neck arched backward. "Oh, God, oh, God," Clarissa screamed, a kind of wild panic in the sound, and he thrust forward quickly, again and again. Now her short, gasped cries echoed in his every thrust and she rose up to meet him each time, her every movement a spasmodic explosion of ecstasy. He felt himself unable to hold back as she arched upwards and hung there. Her cry spiraled in the air, a quivering sound that signaled the wild peak of pleasure. He held tight to her as she trembled and finally, despair in her sobbed cry, fell backward, tiny moaned sounds coming from her mouth, which was still pressed against his chest.

He bent his head, his lips finding her breasts, holding it there, and she uttered small grateful sobs until finally he drew back and found her hazel eyes wide, staring at him almost with an air of incomprehension. "Too little and too much," she murmured.

"You sorry?" he slid at her, and she shook her head at once.

"Oh, no . . . no. It just all seemed to run away with me," Clarissa said as he rested half across her. "Is it always like that?"

"At the end," he told her. "But you hurried it. You became a wild thing."

She pushed onto one elbow, kissed him, and fell back again and pressed his hand around one breast. "You leave a pot simmer too long it finally boils over," she said. "I'm glad it was you who made that happen."

"So am I," he said, and she put one hand behind his neck and drew his face down to her breasts.

"Make it happen again, Fargo," she said.

He smiled as he circled the pink tip with his tongue and heard her soft cry of delight. New discoveries were to be enjoyed with new eagerness. His hand slid down across her strong body and this time he slowed the exploding wildness in her. She writhed and tossed with him with a new delight until, at last, she screamed with sheer ecstasy of pleasure alone and clung to him afterward with exhausted satisfaction. She fell asleep in his arms and woke only when the new sun pushed its way through the hawthorn. She watched him wash and dress, studying his body as though she wanted to imprint every inch of it in her mind, and when he finished, she rose and stood naked in front of him, a newfound boldness in her hazel eyes.

"Not what you're thinking," she said. "I haven't suddenly become a hussy." His laugh held a seed of admission in it. "I want you to remember, too. I want you to come back to me, no matter what happens."

"It may be a while," he said grimly.

"I'll wait." Her eyes held his and he knew she wanted to ask more, but she didn't. The quiet strength he had seen in her ran deep, and as his eyes moved across her loveliness, he knew he didn't want to leave. But he would. Once again, the decision had been made for him. He waited till she slipped into the nightgown, walked her halfway back to the tents, and then swung onto the pinto.

He rode north, knowing other eyes would be watching for him. He'd gone perhaps an hour's riding when the two Pawnee warriors appeared, each with a lance. He moved toward them as they slowly rode away, fell in behind them, and glimpsed the third half-naked rider slip from the trees to follow at his rear.

The sun was in the noon sky when he rode into the Pawnee camp. His escort had closed in around him again. Red Buffalo looked up from where he sat outside his tepee and Fargo's eyes took in the lay of the camp again as the braves watched him with stony faces. He swung to the ground in front of the chief, and the man's massive head was expressionless.

"The great Pawnee chief was right. I could not make the Major listen," Fargo said. "I will do what you want."

"You will free Moonglow and bring her here," the Indian said.

"It may take time. It will not be easy," Fargo said.

Red Buffalo held up one hand and spread his fingers. "Five moons," he said.

"I may fail," Fargo said.

"I will know that if you do not return."

"If that happens?"

"I will begin to kill the hostages, one a day, as I said I would," Red Buffalo answered.

"Let me see the prisoners again," Fargo said, and the Indian shrugged as he led the way past the tepee. Fargo's gaze moved across the line of bound prisoners and paused at Ada. They seemed essentially the same. None had been beaten. The situation was unchanged, and he turned to the chief. "What happens when I bring back Moonglow?" he asked.

"I told you."

"I want to hear the words again."

"I will let the prisoners go. You can take them from here," Red Buffalo said.

Fargo's eyes narrowed in thought for a moment. He knew the shame of a broken promise. The chief would not want that on his name, but he was clever and he had shown his ability to manipulate. Fargo decided he'd not be taken in by the unsaid. "You give your word I can take the prisoners from here. That is not enough," Fargo said, and saw the Indian's coal-black eyes grow smaller. "I want your word that your warriors will not attack us on the way back," Fargo said.

Red Buffalo's eye bored into him. "Fargo is not a man of trust," he said.

"Fargo knows the cunning of Red Buffalo," the Trailsman said, and saw a look of sullenness slide across the massive face.

The Indian waited a long moment before he replied. "My warriors will not attack you on the way back," he said in an icy monotone, and Fargo congratulated himself for his distrust.

He turned and walked away with the Pawnee at his heels. He swung into the saddle and Red Buffalo raised his hand and spread out his fingers again. Fargo nodded and put the Ovaro into a walk as he weaved his way through the Indian camp. The three braves rode with him when he left, back to where they had picked him up. Dusk had begun to slide over the hills.

It was night when he reached the stockade, and his gaze scanned the guardhouse again. He had halted but stayed in the saddle when Duvall stepped from his office and paused before him.

"Haven't seen you around all day," the major said. "Thought maybe you decided to go back to General Leeds."

"That'd take too long. I want to stop a bloodbath of innocent people," Fargo said. "You could do it in five minutes."

"I'm going to do it." Duvall smiled. "But my way. And you can see it happen. You can ride along and watch."

"Ride along?"

"I'm moving the little Pawnee bitch down to the federal prison at Fort Garland," Duvall said, glee in his voice. "I'm taking my whole complement of men, of course. The damn Indian will know it; his scouts will be watching and they'll report back to him. He can't afford to let me get her to Fort Garland. He'll come charging down to save her and I'll cut him to bits. You can hang back and watch."

"When?" Fargo asked.

"We roll tomorrow," the major said, then turned on his heel and walked into the office.

Fargo rode slowly from the stockade, passed Clarissa's tent without stopping, and dismounted when he reached the low hills. He stretched out his bedroll and tried to hold down the excitement that whirled inside him. He had no right to the feeling. He'd no right for optimism. The task was still almost impossible. But Major Duvall was about to hand him the opportunity he sought. Freeing Moonglow from a prison wagon, no matter how well she was guarded, had to offer a better chance for success than trying to free her from the impenetrable guardhouse.

And the major's predictions about Red Buffalo were almost right. Almost, Fargo grunted grimly. The Pawnee chief would know his daughter was in the prison van with a full complement of troops surrounding it. But he wouldn't attack. He'd sweat fish oil, but he'd hold back. He'd let the days go by until he was certain something had gone wrong. But he'd wait, and that was what mattered, Fargo reflected with his eyes narrowed in thought. He'd need time to pick and choose: the right moment, the right spot, the little things that so often spelled the difference between success and failure. He went to sleep knowing that the die was cast now, irrevocably. There was no time left for searching one's soul, for feeling manipulated, for trying to find a way out of the dilemma. Time was a luxury that had vanished.

Fargo went to sleep, had a fitful night, and woke with a new sun. He rode back to the stockade and saw that the troop was ready to ride. A long double-row of brown mounts neatly lined up, a trooper beside each one. He found Duvall half-surrounded by the settlers from the tents and caught Clarissa's glance as he rode up. "You're taking your whole troop and leaving us here? Hell, that's asking the Pawnee to slaughter us," a man said to the major.

"Army business," Duvall said peremptorily.

"Army business is to protect us," the man answered.

"I'm leaving ten men here at the post," the major said.

"Ten men don't mean shit," someone else called out.

"You'll be safe. Red Buffalo is going to be watching me. He's not even going to be thinking about you," Duvall answered.

Fargo saw Clarissa's eyes search his face and his nod was in support of the major's words. She whispered to Howie Atkins, who whispered to someone else, and Fargo heard the rumble of protest begin to die down.

The major turned from the settlers, waved toward the stockade, and Fargo watched as six troopers rode out with the black prison van. A square, box-like wagon, it had a barred window on each side and a narrow door at the back. A small platform at the rear allowed two troopers to stand in front of the door as the van moved. A single trooper held the reins of an army mount with some draft-horse blood in him.

Major Duvall positioned the prison van exactly in the center of the column of troops, swung onto his mount, and cast a glance at Fargo. "You riding along with us or hanging back?" he asked.

"I'll hang back," Fargo said.

"Figured as much," Duvall sneered. "You ride with us and it could be dangerous. You'll be in the middle of it when they come at us."

The major sent his mount forward to the head of the column, barked orders, and the line of cavalry began to move forward in perfect discipline.

Fargo nodded to Lieutenant Baker as the young officer passed, and received a shrug. The last of the column passed him and he turned the Ovaro and rode after it, aware of Clarissa's eyes following him. He swung into the low hills where he could see the column and the prison van with ease, and he parelleled the procession.

The major set a leisurely pace, and by mid-afternoon Fargo knew that Red Buffalo was watching the line of troopers. He couldn't see the chief and his warriors but they were there, in the high hills. It was a certainty.

When dusk came, Duvall halted near a small pond at the bottom of a hill, and Fargo watched the troopers set up camp in quick, efficient army style. The prison van was kept in the center of the camp, he noted, two troopers at the rear door the only direct guards. Major Duvall obviously felt that the rest of his troopers bivouacked all around it was more than enough protection. Ordinarily he'd be right, Fargo conceded, and watched as six sentries surrounded the encampment. He dismounted when night fell and watched the camp cooking fire burn until supper ended and the small flame was doused.

Fargo chewed on the beef jerky in his saddlebag and lay down on his bedroll. He had already decided to let at least one more day go by to see if the major made any changes in his routine. When morning arrived, the Trailsman followed the column southward as it traveled at the same leisurely pace. Duvall was in no hurry. He wanted to bait Red Buffalo, force him to attack out of fury instead of caution. Fargo smiled. The major was doomed to disappointment.

When night came again, Fargo halted closer to the encampment, his eyes sweeping the scene. Duvall hadn't changed the routine, he noted and he sat back and watched the camp grow silent. Fargo had positioned each of the sentries in his mind and he waited till the night hours grew long before he rose and led the pinto into a cluster of bur oak, set out his bedroll, and slept. Two nights had told him enough. It was highly unlikely the major would vary anything, but the third night would confirm it. If he were right, he'd be ready.

He closed his eyes and slept soundly until morning. The troopers hadn't broken camp yet when he rode out, crossed to the other side of the hill and down to the moist land that bordered a stream.

The column would be easy enough to follow when he was ready, and he'd catch up to them even if they rode almost a full day ahead of him. But he quickly found what he looked for: thick rows of elberberry bushes in the moist soil. He took off his shirt, tied the ends together, and began to fill it to overbrimming with the berries. He filled his shirt twice and put the first batch in a hole he scooped out of the soft earth. When he had gathered enough of the juicy berries, he emptied his canteen, dug another smaller hole, and began to use a rock to crush handfuls of the berries.

He had observed Indian women of various tribes do it, and he began to appreciate how long the task took. The crushed berries made a black dye the Indians used to color their hair even blacker than it normally was, and to dye strands of grass and hide to be used in basket designs and clothing decoration. Fargo paused every half-hour to pour the dye into his canteen until, when the sun was in the late afternoon sky, he had gathered enough and his canteen was filled to the top. He washed his hands in the stream and swung into the saddle.

The tracks of the column were fresh and clear enough for a child to pick up, and Fargo rode at a fast canter until the night descended. He slowed and picked his way along after the hoofprints until he saw the small, distant orange flame of the cooking fire. He rode onto a hillock, drew closer until the bivouac was well in sight: the prison van in its usual place, the two sentries at the back door.

Fargo watched the camp bed down and the sentries take up their posts at the perimeter. He swung from the horse and began to undress. He put his clothes atop the saddle and hung the reins loosely over the low branch of an oak. Naked, he poured the dye from the canteen into his cupped hands and began to rub it all over his body. He had used up almost everything in the canteen when he finished, but he was a black wraith, his body covered with the dye from head to toe, an invisible figure in the dark night. He began to move toward the camp in quick, crouched movements, and when he drew near, he dropped to the ground and began to crawl.

He moved toward the nearest sentry, silent and invisible as a black racer slithering toward its prey.

He slowed his crawl and moved forward by inches, the sentry not more than six feet away. The trooper leaned the stock of his rifle on the ground, a faintly bored expression on his face as his eyes peered out toward the dark bulk of the nearest hill. He neither heard nor saw the black shape at his feet until it was too late.

Fargo's arm struck upward, the side of his hand flat and rigid as it smashed into the soldier's neck from the side, and the sentry went limp at once. Fargo caught him and his rifle before either hit the ground and he laid the man on his back and felt his pulse. It was there and Fargo grunted silently in satisfaction.

He dropped to the ground again, the sentry's rifle at his side as he began to crawl toward the prison van. He passed four clumps of sleeping troopers, men who had ridden all day and were hard asleep. It seems hours before he reached the black van, but he knew it had been but minutes. The two soldiers outside the rear door were equipped only with side-arms and were talking to each other in low voices. Fargo crawled almost to the feet of the nearest trooper when, tensing his every muscle, he jumped upward with the rifle swinging in a short arc. It smashed into the nearest soldier's head and he went down. His companion whirled, frozen in surprise for a second. Fargo's hands were around his throat in that second, pressing hard before the man could make a sound. He went limp in moments and Fargo let him slide to the ground.

It had been silent and both men were alive, but they'd not come around for at least five minutes. Fargo reached into the pocket of the nearest one and found the large iron key that fitted the door of the van. He turned the key, carefully pulled the narrow door open, and made out the dark form huddled inside. He stepped into the van and Moonglow rose and he clapped a hand over her mouth and put one finger to his lips, held her there until she nodded understanding. He examined her with his hands in the van. She wore only a deerskin dress, no beads, no jewelry, nothing to rattle.

He stepped to the door of the van and peered out. The camp still slept, a few snoring sounds and nothing more. He lay down on the ground on his belly and motioned for the girl to do the same. She hesitated a moment, then followed his example. He beckoned to her as he began to inch his way across the ground. He paused every few inches to listen and glance behind him. She was at his heels, prone, crawling after him. He felt the beads of perspiration on his brow as he passed the last cluster of sleeping figures. He continued to inch forward, past the inert figure of the sentry, saw that Moonglow still followed close behind, and he continued to crawl. He didn't sit up till he was at the bottom of the hill, where he waited for the girl to catch up to him.

He saw the first, tentative streaks of light touching the sky and he rose to his feet. Moonglow pushed to her feet beside him. He noticed that some of the dye had been smeared away, but he was still mostly a black figure in the darkness. The moon had gone behind the distant hills and the night was at the stygian hour just before dawn. Moonglow a dark shape beside him, he found the Ovaro, helped her onto the horse, and climbed into the saddle behind her, the deerskin dress pressing against his nakedness.

He rode west over the hills. The new day had just begun to break when he spotted a fast-running stream. He halted and swung to the ground. He took a towel from his saddlebag and tossed it at the edge of the stream as he plunged into the cold water and felt himself shiver. He glanced at the girl as she sat silently on the Ovaro, waiting and watching as he stretched out in the stream, turned himself over and then over again as he rubbed his skin. The dye began to slide from him, slowly at first, then quickly, and he was drying himself off as the sun came over the hills. He wrapped the towel around his groin as he stepped from the stream and began to dress.

He could see Moonglow really for the first time. She seemed older than he'd expected, her waist thickening, but that came early to Indian women. She wasn't particularly attractive, but then he had no right to form conclusions.

He took his canteen and washed it clean in the stream. It took a half-dozen rinses to get all the elderberry dye out, but finally he filled it with good, clear water and straightened up. By now all hell had broken loose at the camp. Fargo smiled. And by now Red Buffalo was aware that his daughter was no longer a captive from the eruption in the bivouac and was probably on his way back to his own camp.

Fargo strode to the Ovaro and looked up at the young woman. "I will take you back to your father," he said.

She made no reply except finally a short nod. She seemed fearful, certainly distrustful. But, hell, he couldn't blame her for that. She'd just been stolen from one set of white men by another. She had to be nervous about what it all meant.

He swung onto the pinto behind her and began to move higher into the hills. It would be a long journey back to the Pawnee camp. Moonglow rode in silence and stayed by herself when he halted to rest and freshen up. He was content with that and the fact that she didn't protest when he elected to ride most of the night to make up time.

The next morning he was feeling the drag of exhaustion; even the pinto was moving slowly. Fargo looked up and saw the two Pawnee warriors high on a ridge. They turned and rode along with him, halting when he did to rest. When he catnapped for an hour they were still there on the high ground, showing no effort to make contact. It was well into the afternoon when he began to recognize familiar places in the terrain and the two braves descended to ride in front of him. He followed, and dusk had not begun to cast itself over the land when he found himself riding through the dense stand of black oak and finally the Pawnee camp unfolded itself in front of him.

Fargo allowed a deep sigh to escape his lips, partly relief and partly exhaustion.

Red Buffalo was standing outside his tepee, three braves beside him, when Fargo rode up, dismounted, and gave Moonglow a helping hand down from the horse. He turned, faced the massive head of the Pawnee chief, and saw the Indian bark at the three braves beside him. They leapt forward and Fargo had his arms pinned behind his back in a split second. He felt the anger push away initial surprise as he frowned at Red Buffalo.

"We had an agreement. You gave your word," Fargo said. "I free your daughter and bring her to you and I leave with the captives."

"This is not my daughter," Red Buffalo thundered.

6

Fargo felt himself reeling, his mind spinning like tumbleweed in a twister as he stared at the Pawnee chief. The Indian barked commands at his braves. "See how close the bluecoats are," he ordered, and a half-dozen bronzed forms leapt onto their ponies and raced from the camp.

"I wasn't followed. I didn't lead them here," Fargo said, but the Indian's face was made of scorn and fury.

"You break your word. You try to trick Red Buffalo. You will die with the others."

Fargo heard his curses flung into the air. "The son of a bitch. The goddamn stinking bastard," he said as he saw Duvall's sneering face in front of him. The man had tricked him. He had switched the girl in the prison van. He'd plainly wanted insurance that the Indian wouldn't get his daughter even if his braves managed to reach the van. And now he had blown it all apart, everything left in shattered slivers. Not that he'd care, Fargo swore bitterly. His eyes went back to Red Buffalo. It was all over for everyone unless he could make the Indian believe him.

"He tricked us both," Fargo said. "Why would I bring this squaw into the camp? Why would I come with her? So Red Buffalo could kill me?"

"You hope the soldiers will reach here in time to save you," the Indian said.

"No. They are not coming. I was not followed. I did not lead them here," Fargo said.

Red Buffalo spoke to the squaw in rapid-fire Pawnee, too fast for Fargo to follow, and she replied in low, indistinct words. "Give her to the old squaws," the chief said. "They have not had a slave for a long time." As a brave led her away, Red Buffalo turned to Fargo. "Tie him with the others," he ordered.

"Dammit, I freed the squaw. I thought she was your daughter. I brought her here. I kept my word," Fargo insisted, but the chief was striding into his tepee. Fargo was dragged back to the trees, and he watched hope die in the eyes of the wagon-train captives as they saw him. He was tied to one of the trees with rawhide thongs and his gun was yanked from its holster. He hung there with his head bowed, alternating waves of fury and bitter despair sweeping over him. He cursed Duvall for his trickery. The man had no idea what he had caused, but then he wouldn't really care, Fargo reminded himself. Finally he stopped railing at fate and human deceit and stayed wrapped in bitterness. Dusk had begun to seep into the air when he raised his head as two braves approached him.

Fargo found himself frowning in surprise as they cut him loose and marched him past the wagons to the camp, where the massive form of the Pawnee chief stood, his arms folded across his chest. He was brought to face Red Buffalo and the Indian's black-coal eyes bored into him. "The bluecoats did not come. They did not follow your tracks. The squaw said you did not know she was in the wagon. Perhaps you did not lie," the Indian intoned.

"No perhaps about it," Fargo spit out. "I told you I was tricked."

"Moonglow is still a prisoner. I will give you one more chance," the chief said.

"I'll take it," Fargo said.

"Our bargain is the same. The prisoners for my daughter. If you fail this time, there will not be another chance," Red Buffalo said.

Fargo nodded. The second chance was not due to any kindness on the Indian's part, he realized. Red Buffalo still wanted his daughter back without sacrificing all his warriors. He was willing to try once more for that.

A brave brought the Ovaro and Fargo swung into the saddle. "My gun," he said, and at a nod from the chief another brave handed him the Colt. He holstered the gun, turned the pinto, and slowly rode from the camp as night fell.

He hadn't asked about time. The Pawnee chief would hold back again. He had nothing to lose now by letting events play themselves out. But the searing truth of it all burned inside Fargo as he rode unhurriedly through the black oak. If he didn't produce the real Moonglow pretty quickly, the charade would explode in an orgy of killing.

But he felt exhaustion pull at him. He knew he was too tired to act decisively or to think clearly, and he found a soft place beneath a cottonwood, tossed his bedroll on the ground, and was asleep in minutes. He slept in the deep slumber of total exhaustion until the morning sun woke him. He found a stream, washed, and breakfasted on wild plums before he began to ride eastward. He let plans slowly form in his mind as he sorted out possibilities, separated facts from suppositions, and went over what he had left.

Duvall would be back at the stockade now, furious that his trickery had backfired. He'd be even less inclined to listen to reason now. But for all Duvall knew, Fargo mused, he had stolen the squaw, taken her to Red Buffalo, and been killed for it. The major couldn't be sure if he was alive or dead, and perhaps that was to the good. But he had to get into the stockade again, Fargo knew, and he'd need help. Clarissa, he murmured. He'd get to her first. Maybe he could even enlist the help of some of the others with Clarissa. He quickened his pace, decision made, and then slowed. He didn't want to reach the stockade till after night had fallen, so he paused and rested some.

At dusk he took to the saddle again, and the night was full over the land when he came in sight of the stockade. He dismounted as he drew closer and left the Ovaro alongside a scraggly buckthorn, then moved toward the tents on foot. Some of the settlers were still moving about, he saw, and the sentries atop the stockade wall peered into the distant darkness. He found the Atkins tent, parted the flap, and saw Clarissa look up from sorting clothes.

"Oh, God," she breathed. "No, get away from here." He saw Howie Atkins and his wife look up from the other corner of the tent as he pulled Clarissa outside with him. She clung to him for an instant before pushing away. "They're looking for you. Duvall's been here," she said.

"I know they are. That's why I need your help," he said.

"No. Get away from here. Go into the trees. I'll come find you," she said.

"All right, maybe that'd be best," he agreed, and he had started to back from her when a voice cut in.

"That's far enough, mister," it said, and Fargo turned to see three troopers, rifles all aimed at him, advancing toward him. One yanked the Colt from his holster as the other two kept their guns trained on him. "The major was right," one said. "He told us to watch her tent 'round the clock."

Fargo exchanged a glance with Clarissa and saw the despair in her hazel eyes. "My fault," he said to her.

"March, mister," one trooper said, prodding him in the back with a rifle. Fargo marched and the troopers pushed him to the major's office, where Duvall stepped outside, a sneering grin sliding across his face.

"Bring him inside and stand guard at the door," he said. He entered the office as Fargo was pushed into a chair and the troopers retired to stand outside the closed door.

"You bastard," Duvall said. "But I've got you where I want you now. Stealing a United States prisoner. That's an automatic firing squad, Fargo." He leaned back against the wall. "I'll give you credit for one thing: you're good. I didn't think you'd get her out. I expected you'd get yourself shot dead trying, which was the way I planned it."

"You planned it?" Fargo frowned. "You expected I'd try to free the girl?"

"That's right. But you pulled it off without getting yourself filled with lead. Wrong squaw, but you got her out, I'll give you that. You see, I never believed that story about the Pawnee sending for you to bring back a message about the hostages he had. He could've sent that to me any number of ways. I figured he wanted you for something more, such as getting his daughter out." Fargo's frown stayed on the man. Duvall was more astute than he'd given him credit for being. "How long did it take you to know she was a ringer?" the major asked.

"Soon enough," Fargo said carefully.

"You didn't bring her to Red Buffalo or you'd be dead now." Duvall laughed in sneering triumph and Fargo allowed a shrug. He'd let the man continue to think that he'd failed and there was nothing more. It was a small plus, but he was in no position to turn away small favors. "I'm going to have you shot, Fargo, but not until I bring down that damn savage. I want you to see that happen. I might even capture him and have you both shot together."

"That's nice. I think I'd like company while I'm getting shot."

Duvall shouted and the three troopers reentered the room. "Take him to the guardhouse," Duvall said, and saw the moment of surprise touch Fargo's face. "She's not there." He grinned. "But I've got her safe, don't you worry about that. I'm going to give her daddy a second chance to get himself wiped out, sort of an encore performance, you might say."

"Maybe he won't take the bait," Fargo said.

"He'll take it. You won't be around to screw it up," the major said. "Search him carefully," he ordered, and one of the troopers obeyed and finally came onto the calf holster and pulled the blade free. "What do you know?" Duvall smiled. "You're full of surprises, Fargo."

"I try," Fargo said.

"Put him in the guardhouse," Duvall ordered.

"I want to see Clarissa Brown. I want her to take care of my horse. I'm allowed that," Fargo said.

"Lock him up and then let the girl visit," Duvall said, and Fargo was marched from the office. His eyes swept the compound as they took him to the guardhouse and he spotted the prison van parked in the far corner behind the stables. The guardhouse turned out to be a single cell, a square space with one barred window, a candle burning in a wall holder. A washbasin and toilet facility took up one corner and a mattress lay on the floor.

"Clarissa Brown. She's in the last tent to set up," Fargo said. The troopers left and he heard the lock turn in the door. He lowered himself to the mattress and thought about Duvall's remark. The major had been unable to resist gloating and willing to tell him of his plans. He plainly felt secure enough now for that. He was probably right, Fargo swore silently. But the remark about taking Moonglow on another trip had been more than information. It had served as a desperate spur to find a way out of the prison. There was still a chance to avert a bloodbath of innocent lives. A terribly slender chance, yet a chance.

It was perhaps a half-hour later when one of the guards appeared at the barred door, Clarissa beside him, pain in her hazel eyes.

Fargo moved to the bars. He had thought it out as he waited. There was no way he'd be able to sneak to the van again when the troops were bivouacked. Duvall would have sentries posted every few feet apart. There was but one way and one chance, and he had to risk it. The guard stepped back a dozen paces and Fargo spoke in a whisper to Clarissa.

"I told them I wanted to talk to you about taking care of the Ovaro," he said. "I need you to help me get out of here."

The hazel eyes grew wide. "How, in heaven's name?" Clarissa breathed. "I can't smuggle a gun to you. They searched me just now. They'll do it every time I visit. I didn't like it much."

"I know you can't get a gun to me, but I've got to be in that prison van when they move Moonglow," he said.

"In the van?" Clarissa echoed incredulously. "You can't mean that. They'll be bound to see you."

"Most prison vans have a double floor. Under the regular floor is a storage space for prisoner's belongings when they're transporting a van full. They won't be using that for Moonglow," Fargo said.

"It's crazy," Clarissa said. "And I still can't get you out of here."

"You can help me get out," he said. "Listen very carefully and do exactly what I say." Clarissa nodded and he put his face against the bars. "You'll get the Ovaro tomorrow. Bring him to your tent. Then you go to Duvall. Tell him I've given you the horse and my Colt, everything I own. Tell him I know it's over for me. Duvall is feeling smug. He's sure he has everything going his way now. I'm betting he gives you my gun. When he does, you put it in my saddlebag."

"Then, what?" Clarissa asked.

"Duvall will take to the road soon. If I escape, he'll move at once. He'll figure I'm riding to General Leeds," Fargo said. "You come visit me tomorrow night. Put six matches in your hair. They won't search your hair. When you leave, wait outside the stockade gate with the Ovaro."

"All right," Clarissa murmured, and put her lips through the opening between the bars. He pressed his mouth to them and she let the kiss linger for another moment before pulling back. She turned and walked from the guardhouse and the trooper returned to his post outside the outer door.

Fargo lay down on the mattress and slept until he was wakened by the changing of the guard in the morning. He washed and took the coffee they brought him, sipped it slowly as he peered through the barred window. It allowed him only a narrow view of the stockade, but he could see troopers grooming their mounts and polishing gear. They were preparing to ride out within a day, he guessed. Duvall would insist on everything shining, every buckle in place. A soldier should look smart when he dies. Fargo flung a curse through the barred window, turned away, and stretched out on the mattress.

He used sleep as a refuge and let the day go by. A plate of beans and a slice of buffalo meat was served him as supper. He ate, not out of hunger but for the need of a meal inside him. But with the night the hours seemed to go more quickly, and he was ready when the trooper came to the barred door. "Somebody to see you," he announced, and Fargo rose as Clarissa appeared. She wore her hair up atop her head in a kind of bun, he noted.

"How'd it go?" he asked in a whisper as she reached the bars.

"The major gave me your gun, after he took the bullets out," she said. "You were right. He's feeling smug."

"The Ovaro?" Fargo asked.

"He'll be waiting outside the gate," Clarissa said. "What happened the first time? You never told me."

"I can't now, but Duvall outfoxed me," he answered.

She put her lips through the space between the bars again and he tasted the warm sweetness of her in his mouth. "Be careful," she said. "Come back to me."

"I aim on doing just that." He smiled. She lifted one hand to the top of her head and seemed to pull out hairpins and her hair came tumbling down.

"I've had it up all day," she said in a voice loud enough for the trooper to hear as she pushed her hand through the bars, her body blocking the guard's vision. Fargo took the six long wooden matches and pushed them into his pocket. "I'll be going now," Clarissa said, and gave him another kiss through the bars.

"Thanks for coming," he told her, and watched her tall, strong figure walk away, the trooper beside her hardly an inch taller. Fargo sank back on the mattress, stretched out, and let the night grow deeper. When the night was halfway to dawn, he rose, struck two of the matches against each other, and held the flame to the edge of the mattress. He struck two more and put the lighted tips to the other corner of the mattress. The material didn't catch fire in a blaze of flame, but he hadn't expected that. It began to do just what he wanted: burn slowly, almost smolder, and immediately begin to send off waves of thick, foul-smelling smoke. Before it filled the cell, Fargo hurried to the heavy porcelain washbasin, emptied it, and took a firm grip on one edge.

As the smoke began to fill the room, his breath starting to become gasping sounds, he shouted and banged on the cell door. In moments he heard the voices and shouts of consternation. Three voices, he picked out as he flattened himself against one wall and dropped to one knee where the smoke was not yet as thick as in the rest of the cell. "Get me out of here," he shouted, and heard the lock of the door being opened.

"Stay back," the trooper who entered shouted, and Fargo heard the man cough at once. "Jesus, get the fire buckets," the man gasped. Fargo saw the shape of a second trooper enter while he heard the third racing away. "Where the hell are you, mister?" the first trooper called as he took another tentative step, tried to peer through the thickening billows of foul smoke, and coughed hard again.

"Here," Fargo said as he straightened up and

107

swung the heavy porcelain washbasin. It smashed into the trooper's head and he went down. Fargo caught his rifle before it hit the floor. He glimpsed the second trooper starting to run from the cell, bent over and coughing. Fargo met him halfway out the door, poked the rifle into his ribs and the man halted in fear and surprise. "Drop the gun," the Trailsman said, and the soldier let the rifle clatter to the floor. He had a sidearm, Fargo saw, and yanked the army-issue Smith & Wesson five-shot, single-action revolver from its holster.

"Outside," Fargo ordered and, walking close to the soldier, marched the man from the guardhouse, which was now beginning to fill with smoke from the cell. He held the revolver into the soldier's ribs as they passed a dozen troopers running with fire buckets. "Very good," he said quietly. "I don't want to hurt you. I won't, unless you make me."

"No, sir, I won't do that," the soldier said as Fargo reached the gate of the stockade. Shouts and more running feet echoed from behind him, and he glanced back to see Duvall, in a robe, come from his quarters and stare at the guardhouse. A soldier was posted at the gate and Fargo muttered to the trooper as they neared.

"Tell him to open up," he said, and the trooper nodded.

"Open up, soldier. I've got to take this man outside," the trooper said, and Fargo waited as the sentry lifted the big, wooden latch from the gate. He took the trooper with him outside, paused, and searched the night until he spotted the Ovaro, a half-dozen yards away. He kept the trooper with him till he reached the horse and swung into the saddle. Removing the bullets from the Smith & Wesson, he tossed it back to the trooper.

"Here," he said. "I know the army takes it out of

your pay if you lose your gun." He slammed his heels into the Ovaro's side and the horse raced off in an instant gallop. As he passed the tent, he glimpsed the tall figure standing outside, watching, and he waved an arm and raced into the night. He rode perhaps a half-mile into a thicket of oak and halted. He found his Colt in the saddlebag and reloaded with the cartridges from his gun belt.

Duvall would be aware of the escape by now, Fargo mused with a grim smile. He'd be beside himself with fury, but he'd feel certain his escaped prisoner was racing for General Leeds. He'd take his prison van out first thing in the morning, that was a certainty. Fargo found himself wondering where he was keeping Moonglow. Perhaps tied and under guard in his quarters, Fargo speculated. It was unimportant. She'd be under too heavy a guard to get to now.

What was important was that Duvall would settle his men down for the remainder of the night so they'd be ready to ride, come morning. He'd call off all his extra guards and let them get some sleep. The fox had escaped and there was nothing to be done about that now. Fargo smiled as he turned the Ovaro and slowly began to ride back toward the stockade. The fox had escaped, but he was not running.

He walked the horse most of the way and circled to approach the stockade from the rear, where a line of tall hackberry rose some ten feet from the wall of the compound. He dismounted, scanned the stockade rear wall, the hand-hewn timbers uneven at the top. No sentries, he had already noted, and he found a place where there was an uneven space between the wood at the top. There was but one thing more to do before he scaled the wall, and he left the Ovaro tethered in the thick hackberry and edged his way around the stockade, his back pressed to the wall, where he was out of sight of the sentries above.

When he rounded the front of the stockade where the tents stretched out in an uneven half-circle, he moved slowly from the wall, almost casually. The sentries atop the front wall saw only the indistinct figure of one of the settlers moving among the tents. He reached the Atkins tent, slipped through the flap, and found Clarissa's sleeping form nearest. He took one silent step and pressed his hand over her mouth; she woke at once, a moment of fear in her eyes until she focused on him. He drew his hand back and she tiptoed from the tent with him.

"You up for one more thing?" he asked, and she nodded.

"You know it," she said.

"Duvall will lead the squad out, come morning. He'll take the same road he did last time. It's the best one for him. I want you to follow him. I'm going to need a horse if I pull it off," Fargo said. "I left the Ovaro in the hackberry behind the stockade. Take your mount and bring him along."

"I have it." Clarissa nodded.

"You'll find Duvall's trail will wind through low passages bordered by hills. You stay in the hills. You'll be able to see the column without any problem. They stop; you stop. They camp; you camp. You'll know it if I get out with Moonglow. You'll hear the commotion. You stay in the hills and I'll find you."

"All right," she said.

He drew her to him. "If Ada gets out of this alive, she'll have you to thank as much as me," he said.

"I wouldn't say that." Clarissa smiled.

"I'll have to find a way to thank you afterward. You've been something special," he said.

"I know just how you can do that," she said, and a tiny smile came to her lips.

"Count on it," he said, and Clarissa's face grew sober as her arms encircled his neck.

"Come back. It seems that's all I keep saying these nights," she murmured.

"Keep saying it," he replied, and met her mouth with his until he finally pulled away.

She strolled with him until he was below the line of vision of the sentries and watched him hurry on into the night.

When Fargo returned to the rear wall of the stockade, he took his lariat from the Ovaro and sent it spinning upward to the uneven space at the top of the wall. He felt it catch, pulled it tight, tested it, and felt the secure tautness before he began to pull himself up. He halted when he reached the top, clung there with both arms holding on to the wood, and drew in deep breaths as he surveyed the compound below. It was a silent, dark place, no one patrolling outside the guardhouse. The distant sentries on the walkway of the front wall were the only figures in sight, both their backs to him.

Fargo pulled himself up, one leg over the top, and brought the lariat up with him and dropped it down over the other side of the wall. When it reached the ground, he began to lower himself down, letting himself slide down as quickly as he could without burning his hands on the rope. Once on the ground, he jiggled the lariat until it came free at the top and tumbled into his hands. Moving in a half-crouch, he darted to where the prison van rested, a black shape in the darkness. He opened the narrow rear door and felt along the floorboard of the van until he found the small indentation where it met the side panel. He curled his fingers into the spot and pulled, and the floorboard came up. He peered at the storage space that was the double floor.

He reached down and ran his fingers over the second floor, feeling for what he finally found, cracks in the wood and spaces where the floor met the corners of the van. There'd be enough air filtering in to keep him from suffocating and he began to lower himself into the storage space. He found he had to lie on his back and stretch out to stay flat enough to fit into the space. When he settled down, he reached up and pulled the top floorboard down over himself and the black night became stygian. He lay in the silence as the world disappeared and he felt as though he were entombed. But the faint, filtered air that found its way through the floorboard cracks told him that space and time did exist, and he drew sleep around himself with grateful reassurance.

The jouncing woke him, then the voices, and he heard the rattle of the harness gear. They were hitching the horse to the van. The next sound that came to him was footsteps on the floorboard atop him. He heard the van door slammed shut, and the footsteps became small, shuffling sounds and then fell silent. But Moonglow was above him, only inches away. The lives of many innocent people lay within his reach, so close and yet so far. If he could escape with the girl, that should be the end of it. Only it wouldn't be. He'd known that all along. But freeing Moonglow was the key to it. Without that, nothing else had a chance.

He pushed aside further thoughts and listened to the sounds that drifted dimly to him from outside, the beat of the horses' hooves, the creak of the van wheels, an ocassional hard bump, and the commands barked down the line of the column from time to time. Duvall called a halt once in midmorning and another in midafternoon. When the prison van drew to a halt for the third time, Fargo heard the sounds of horses being moved away and the rattle of bits and bridles being removed. They were bivouacking for the night. He strained his ears but heard only murmured voices from the front of the van. They were leaving the horse harnassed for the night.

Fargo's eyes narrowed in the stygian blackness. A new option had just presented itself, perhaps better than any other. Sometimes noise, boldness, and surprise were far better weapons than stealth.

He stretched the muscles of his body to ease the stiffness that had come with his unmoving, cramped position. The sounds from outside, low voices, the clatter of tin plates, finally died away, and there was only silence. He knew he dared not move too soon. Some men took time to sleep soundly, and he counted minutes into hours until finally he knew the moment was at hand. Softly, he tapped upon the floorboard over him, tapped again, a gentle rapping, and he heard the shuffle of steps. The sound stopped and he tapped again and heard the footsteps move to a corner of the van.

He reached up with both hands, pressed his palms against the floorboard and pushed with slow deliberation. It rose, lifted half upright, and he sat up and peered across the van to the dark shape huddled in one corner.

"Red Buffalo has sent me to take you home," Fargo said, and lowered the floor back in place as he climbed out. He took a step toward the dark shape. "Do you understand me?"

"Who are you?" she asked.

"Someone your father sent. Fargo," he said. "I

am going to take you out of here." She made no reply but he could feel her digesting his words. "You must do exactly as I say," he told her. "Do you understand?"

She waited a moment before answering. "Yes," she murmured finally.

"Come here," he said, and reached out. She let him take her arm and he drew her to the rear door of the van. He made a knocking motion with his fist, and she nodded. He drew the Colt as she stepped to the door, had it upraised and poised to strike as the girl tapped on the door. She paused, then tapped again, and he heard the murmur of voices from outside. He tensed arm muscles as the door was opened and the face of a young trooper peered into the van. Fargo swung around and brought the barrel of the Colt down on the man's head with one motion, took a half-step forward, and smashed it against the temple of the second guard, who was still staring in surprise at his companion. "Out," he hissed at Moonglow, and yanked her from the wagon.

She landed lightly on both feet and he had only time to glimpse a black-haired, slender form in a deerskin dress as he raced to the front of the wagon with her. He leapt into the driver's seat and she followed beside him. Holding the reins with his left hand, the Colt with his right, he roared a shout as he snapped the reins over the horse. The animal surged forward, and with another hard snap of the reins he put the horse into a hard-driving gallop.

Shouts of alarm split the air and he glimpsed figures waking, pushing to their feet as he sent the van careening through the center of the camp. A half-dozen troopers dived out of his way, leaping up from their blankets as the van thundered at them. But he was nearing the edge of the encampment, and the sentries at the perimeter had turned and were firing.

"Stay down," he yelled at Moonglow as bullets thudded into the side of the van. He fired the Colt back at three blue-uniformed figures running toward him, and saw them duck away. But the van was racing out of the camp now and he kept the horse in a straight line as he headed for a deep stand of black oak. He shot a glance backward and saw the camp was still in disarray, with a dozen figures running for where their mounts were tethered. But he had a hundred yards on them already and he drove the horse on as the line of oak rose up in front of him. He held the horse in line for another ten yards and then dropped the reins.

"Jump," he yelled at the girl as he leapt from his side of the van. He caught a blurred glimpse of her diving from the other side as he hit the ground, rolled, and saw the horse veer off before smashing into the trees. Moonglow was on one knee as he reached her and pulled her up. "Run. This way," he said, and raced into the thick stand of oak. He ran a straight line, then twisted, and she stayed with him with ease. She was an Indian girl, he reminded himself, and had run through forests all her young life. He heard the shouts and the sound of horses galloping as he climbed a low hill in the oak.

But the night was black, the forest impossible for fast riding, and most important, they hadn't any idea which way he had fled. They'd race their mounts back and forth and finally realize the futility of it all and return to camp. Fargo smiled as he thought about Duvall, and he wished he were able to see the major's livid face. But he had still other plans for Duvall, none of which would make him happy.

Fargo continued up the hill for another hundred yards and found a half-circle with a soft cover of star moss. "Sleep," he said to Moonglow as he stretched out. She curled up at once, still only a slender shape in the darkness, and he let a deep breath escape him as he closed his eyes. It would be simple enough to take her back to her father. That would complete the bargain. It would also be a mistake, he realized. He had become increasingly convinced of that with every meeting with Red Buffalo.

He had dealt with Duvall's uncaring, compassionless ambition. Now he had to deal with the implacable hate that lay behind the Pawnee chief's manipulative cleverness.

7

Morning brought a hot sun and Fargo's first real look at Moonglow as she rose and brushed her long black hair back. He saw a young girl's face, even-featured, attractive in a quiet, contained way, with more boldness in it than most Indian women showed. The results of being a chief's daughter, he decided.

Her round black eyes studied him, a tiny furrow touching her brow. "Why did my father send you?" she asked.

"Because I had the best chance of getting to you," Fargo answered, and turned his eyes from her to peer down the hill through the trees. He could see the camp below, tiny figures moving about, preparing to return to the stockade. They had brought the prison van back into the camp, he saw. He turned to look at Moonglow as she suddenly began to walk up the hillside. His eyes followed her path and he saw the glint of the sun on the stream a dozen yards on. She halted at the stream, shed the deerskin dress in one, quick motion, and stepped into the water beautifully naked.

He watched her, a slender figure, small breasts with light-brown nipples that stood firm and matched the rest of her figure perfectly. He took in a flat abdomen, an almost smooth pubic triangle, and lean, lithe legs. She stretched out in the stream, a doelike quality to her as the water glistened on her faintly copper skin. No immodesty, just simple naturalness, he realized, and he turned away from her with an effort.

His gaze went back to the bottom of the hill, where the tiny figures were starting to break camp. His eye drew a line from where Major Duvall had encamped during the night, up into the hills a little behind the spot. Clarissa was in that area somewhere, he thought as he pulled himself up into the nearest oak.

He climbed above the low branches until he had a commanding, falcon's view of the hilly area to his left. Slowly, his eyes moved across one level, then another, and then still another, scanning back and forth, searching for the telltale movement of leaves, the swaying of branches. He had swept the area for the third time when suddenly he saw it—movement in the tree cover—and he focused on the spot. The movement became a horse, then a figure in a brown dress. He made a mental note of the spot and climbed from the tree as Moonglow returned in the deerskin dress.

"This way," he told her, and she followed as he went into a long-legged, loping stride across the hillside, staying well in the tree cover. Though half his size, Moonglow kept up with him without drawing a long breath, he noted.

Far below, the column had begun the ride back to the stockade and Fargo saw the trees on the hillside quiver more strongly. Clarissa and the two horses were moving restlessly as she watched the column move on. He told her he'd find her. She'd remember that. But she would still be apprehensive, aware of the chance that something might have gone wrong in the escape. Dozens of shots were fired. He increased his pace, broke into a run

118

as he kept his eyes fixed on the spot where Clarissa waited.

As the column moved on, he risked moving into clear space to make up time, and finally he was bearing down on the cluster of trees. He saw Clarissa step into the open, her face filling with happy excitement as she saw him, and he cast a quick glance at Moonglow.

The Indian girl was still at his heels. She came to a stop only when he did, and dropped to one knee as he embraced Clarissa. He pulled back to see Moonglow watching him with her eyes narrowed. "You said you were taking me home," she remarked, a touch of imperiousness in her tone.

"I am," he said. "My way. My time." She settled herself down on the grass and he moved out of earshot with Clarissa. "I think Red Buffalo is going to cross me up," he said.

"I thought you had a pact, an agreement," Clarissa said.

" 'My warriors will not attack you on the way back,' " he said," Fargo quoted.

"You think he'll break that promise?"

"No. He'll keep it as he understands it, and I'm afraid of what that might mean. How far is the way back? All the way to the compound? Or only the few miles nearest his camp? Is the way back halfway to the compound?" Fargo asked. "He's going to interpret that promise his way. But he's not going to let all those settlers go free to encroach more on Indian land."

"You're keeping your end of the agreement and he'll bend his to suit himself, that's what you're saying. Duvall and he are the same," Clarissa said.

"Not at all. Duvall will do anything for himself. Red Buffalo will do anything for his people. Duvall wants; Red Buffalo hates. There's no contest. Duvall will crack; Red Buffalo won't," Fargo said.

"What can you do? You have to bring the girl back," Clarissa asked.

"Yes, but after I take the reins out of Duvall's hands. Then I'll see if I can keep Ada and the others alive," Fargo said, and cast a glance at Clarissa's mount. "You have your rifle with you," he said. "Good. You're going to stay here with her until I get back." He turned to Moonglow, took a length of lariat from his saddle, and began to tie her wrists together.

"You lied," she accused.

"No, I'll take you back. There's just been a delay, and I want to make sure you don't go running off," he told her, and left enough slack in the rope for her to lower herself to the ground.

"When will you be back?" Clarissa asked.

"Tonight," he said.

She took her rifle from its saddle case as he climbed onto the Ovaro. She settled herself down facing Moonglow while he rode away into the hill country.

Night had fallen before Fargo drew near to the stockade. He circled in the trees until he was once again at the rear wall, unseen in the dense hackberry. He let the night deepen, and when the moon reached the midnight sky, he dismounted, took his lariat, and approached the wall. There was no need to search for a spot atop the wall this time, and he tossed the rope onto the place he had used but a few nights before. He pulled himself up to the top of the wall and paused for a brief moment to scan the inner yard of the stockade. It was a dark and silent place, the troopers hard asleep in their barracks, as he expected they'd be. The two distant sentries at the front wall were the only moving things in the courtyard as they slowly paced the walkway.

He slid down the other side of the wall. It seemed almost a familiar routine now, but this time he passed the empty guardhouse in a crouch, stayed against the wall of the low building that housed the officer's quarters. He knew Duvall's quarters would adjoin his office. When he reached the door, he closed one hand around the knob and turned it very slowly. The door latch hardly clicked as it opened, and he stepped inside and paused to listen. He heard the sound of heavy breathing from the next room, where the faint moonlight through the window was enough to let him see the half-open door. He stepped through it and saw the bulky shape atop a narrow bed.

He drew the Colt as he reached the side of the bed in two long steps. He pressed the end of the revolver barrel against Duvall's throat. "Wake-up time," he said softly.

The major snapped awake, stared upward, blinked, and hissed a curse. A kerosene lamp rested atop a small end table.

"Light the lamp," Fargo said, and kept the gun pressed against Duvall's throat as the man leaned over and turned on the lamp. The soft glow immediately lighted the room and Fargo stepped back but kept the Colt aimed at the major's throat.

"You're crazy coming here, you son of a bitch," Duvall said.

"Get dressed," Fargo ordered, and Duvall's eyes peered hard at him.

"What the hell for?" the man barked.

"Because you don't want to be dead and I'd be happy to oblige you in that because you are a no-good bastard," Fargo said. "That's one reason."

"What's the other?"

"You do exactly what I say and my report to General Leeds will let you put in transfer papers without a court-martial," Fargo said.

"Court-martial? On what grounds?" Duvall blustered, but Fargo caught the nervousness that touched his eyes.

"Inflaming the Indians against your orders to calm the situation. Needlessly attempting to sacrifice your entire squad. Turning your back on two wagonloads of settlers. That'll do for starters," Fargo said.

"You won't shoot me," Duvall said, but there was more bluster than certainty in his tone.

"The hell I won't. It's your life against everybody else's. I don't have a choice, mister," Fargo said. "I need something. I'm going to get it with your help or without it."

Duvall's tongue licked his suddenly dry lips. "The shot'd wake the compound. You'd never get out alive."

Fargo moved with lightninglike speed. He yanked the pillow from the bed and pressed it over Duvall's face with one hand while he pushed the Colt into the pillow with the other. "Guess again," he said as he pulled the hammer back on the gun. He heard Duvall's muffled cries and drew the pillow back.

"All right, all right," the man said, and now the fear in his eyes was very real.

"Get dressed," Fargo ordered again, and this time Duvall hurriedly pulled on his uniform. When he finished, Fargo motioned to the adjoining office and followed the man inside, the gun against his back. Duvall lighted the lamp on the desk and Fargo stepped back a pace, but the Colt stayed unwavering. "Now, take one of those official army pieces of stationary and start writing."

Duvall drew a piece of paper from the desk and

took up the pen beside the inkstand. "Write what?" he muttered.

"Exactly what I'm going to tell you," Fargo said. "Lieutenant Roger Baker. . . . For personal reasons, I am turning command of the post over to you. Give your full cooperation to General Leeds' representative, Mr. Skye Fargo. My signature below makes this an official and proper order." Fargo halted, waited for Duvall to finish. "Now sign it," he said, and he watched the man's signature complete the short note. "Put it in an envelope with the lieutenant's name on it and leave it on the desk," Fargo said, and when Duvall finished, he prodded the man toward the door. "We're going to get your horse first and then take a little ride," he said. "I'm going to let you meet Moonglow again."

He saw surprise come into the major's face and he smiled inwardly. It would help keep the man off-balance. Fargo crossed to the stable and kept the Colt steady on Duvall as the man saddled his mount. "Lead the horse," he said, and stepped close to the major, pushing the Colt into the man's ribs. "One wrong move and your stinking career is over," Fargo muttered, and Duvall's tight face showed that he realized the words were no hollow threat. Staying at his side, the Trailsman walked to the gate.

The sentry's brows lifted when he saw them. "You going outside, Major?" the soldier asked.

Fargo pressed the Colt harder into Duvall's ribs. "Special business," Duvall said.

"You forget to tell the trooper about the letter you left for Lieutenant Baker?" Fargo asked innocuously.

"Tell the lieutenant there's a note in my office for him, come morning," Duvall said, and the sentry lifted the heavy wooden latch bar for the gate to swing open.

Fargo walked out with Duvall, waited till the gate was shut, and then led the man to where he'd left the Ovaro in the hackberry. He swung into the saddle and led the way north into the hills.

"Same rules," Fargo said to him as they rode. "Don't try anything and you might get to see your pension." He rode for a few hours and then pulled to a halt in a stand of smooth sumac and ordered Duvall to dismount. Using his lariat, he tied the major to one of the sumacs, binding him tight from his arms to his ankles.

"Goddamn, you said you were taking me to the Pawnee squaw," Duvall protested.

"Change of heart," Fargo said. "You'll be nice and safe here till someone comes to set you loose. That won't be right away, though."

"You can't leave me here like this," Duvall said.

"Watch me," Fargo tossed back, and swung onto the pinto.

"I'll get you for this, Fargo, for all of it," Duvall shouted, but Fargo was riding back the way he'd come.

He reached the stockade a little after dawn. He rode in as Lieutenant Baker came from Duvall's office, the note in his hand, a furrow on his youthful brow. The furrow became a frown of astonishment as he saw the big black-and-white horse canter to a stop.

"You have the major's orders, I see. Good." Fargo smiled.

"I don't understand this, not any of it. The major gave us orders to shoot you on sight," Baker said, and held up the slip of paper. "And now this."

"He had a change of heart. He saw the light. Sing

hallelujah, Lieutenant," Fargo said. "It's a long story. I'll give you the details when I've time."

The lieutenant peered at him. "Don't play me for a fool, Fargo," he said. "This whole thing stinks."

Fargo let his lips purse as he thought for a long moment. "Duvall's a madman," he said. "He was willing to send all of you to your deaths. He turned his back on two wagons of settlers. I'm trying to save all those innocent people and your whole squad. That's all I'm going to say on that for now."

Baker nodded, his young face grave. "What do you want, Fargo?"

"I made a pact with Red Buffalo. I'm pretty damn sure he's going to try to outfox me on it. I've got to carry through my end to give those wagon people a chance at life. I need you to give them one more chance," Fargo said, and quickly explained his plan. When he finished, Lieutenant Baker was silent for a moment.

"I owe you one, Fargo," he said finally. "I'll turn the men out at once."

"You're doing the right thing," Fargo said, and wheeled the Ovaro around. He waited outside the stockade until the lieutenant rode out at the head of the column. Fargo swung in beside him and led the way north, skirting the stand of sumac where he'd left Duvall. He moved into the low hills, rose higher, and finally came in sight of the hillside where he had left Clarissa. She saw him at the head of the column with the lieutenant and stepped into the open. He shifted direction and drew up to where she waited and saw Moonglow standing nearby.

"You'll stay here," he told Clarissa, and turned to Baker. "You know what to do," he said, and the lieutenant nodded.

"Exactly," he said. "I hope you're guessing right, Fargo."

"That makes the two of us," Fargo said, and wheeled the Ovaro to where Moonglow waited. He leaned down and untied her bonds and pulled her into the saddle in front of him. He exchanged a glance with Clarissa that needed no words, and put the horse into a slow trot. The lieutenant's words rode with him, the grim truth in them an unseen cloak around his shoulders. The last phase of it would indeed be a danger-filled guessing game. He had tried to think as Red Buffalo would, to stay one step ahead of the wily Pawnee chief. But it was a tenuous venture at best. The single all-important question still remained: how long would the Indian wait? How long to keep one's word and keep one's destiny? Fargo grimaced and quickened the Ovaro's pace. He'd have the answer in time, he knew, and he'd have no say in it. He could only hope he had guessed right, as the lieutenant had said.

He spurred the pinto higher into the hills. He'd not approach the Pawnee camp the way he'd come before. Red Buffalo would have his scouts watching for him hours away to escort him in as they had done before. But he'd arrive on his own this time, Fargo grunted. A gesture, he realized, but it would take the chief aback. He'd have to realize that he wasn't as thoroughly in control as he'd believed he was. It had come down to that, Fargo knew, the small and subtle things, the gamesmanship that could result in just enough to spell the difference between life and death. As he reached a high ridge under a line of red cedar, the Indian girl turned to glance at him.

"My father picked well when he chose you," she said, the comment delivered with cool, almost regal appraisal, and once again he was very aware that she was a chief's daughter. "Taking me from the middle of the bluecoats was a great coup."

"Didn't do it for making a great coup," Fargo said.

"Why did you do it?"

"To save the lives of innocent people."

"Mine?"

"Yours, too."

"But really your people," she prodded.

"That's right," he snapped in annoyance at her cool, probing wisdom.

"My father knows what will make his warriors do battle. That's why he is a great chief," Moonglow said with infuriating smugness.

"I'm not one of his warriors, goddammit," Fargo flung back, and realized the galling truth in her comment. He might as well have been, he swore silently. But it wasn't over yet. Red Buffalo would learn that puppets can kick back.

"You are still a great warrior," Moonglow said, and there was no smug prodding in her voice now.

"Thanks," he said, unable to keep the edge of bitterness out of the word.

They had gone perhaps another two hours when the sun sparkling on a mountain pond caught his eye. Moonglow had seen it just as quickly.

"Can we stop?" she asked, and he nodded, shifted direction, and reined up at the pond. They were on high land but not more than another half-hour from the Pawnee camp, he guessed, and he slid from the saddle with the girl.

She knelt at the edge of the pond for a moment and then flung the deerskin dress away and stepped into the cool, refreshing water. He watched her slender, doelike body as she dived, rose to the surface, played in the pond with twists and turns. She was really quite beautiful naked, he observed, small breasts with flat nipples perfect on her, the firm, small rear end equally fitting. He felt the stirring in his loins and the thought that followed.

She suddenly swam to the edge of the pond and climbed out, the droplets of water glistening on her faintly coppery skin, the small, almost hairless pubic mound adding to the childlike quality to her, but the sensuous way she had of standing with her hips thrust forward was all grown woman. She turned, sauntered in front of him, and knelt on the grass, the small breasts provocative twin points. He saw the dark smoldering in her eyes. The hint of a smile touched her lips and the thought in his mind grew with the same speed as the wanting in his loins.

Maybe she was just a natural tease. Or perhaps this was her own kind of revenge for being held captive. To take her would be a very personal blow to the damn Pawnee chief's smug manipulativeness. But he was giving intellectual reasons to justify a very unintellectual urge, he realized. He watched Moonglow lean back on her elbows, her lovely, slender body turned upward as a sunflower turns to the sun. Damn, she was being purposefully provocative, he told himself. He rose and walked over to stand before her. "Aren't you afraid I will take you?" he asked.

"We are taught that it is an honor to be taken by a great warrior," she said. "And only a great warrior can take a chief's daughter." Her black eyes held his, no coyness in her, the sensual provocativeness of her child-woman body emitting its own waves. Maybe, in some strange way, a tribal heritage of arcane origin, she felt a duty. Maybe it was a wanting that grew out of cultural roots he could neither know nor understand. But she was waiting, willing if not offering. The surging inside him spiraled.

"Dammit, honey, you are about to be honored," he muttered, and pulled off clothes until he fell beside her with his own nakedness. He saw her eyes flick over the muscled smoothness of his body and return to his face as he pressed his mouth on hers. She took a moment to respond and then her lips opened, drew him into her mouth, and he felt the palms of her hands pressing against his sides. He took his lips from hers, slid down to draw in one small breast, and felt its soft firmness, the little, flat nipples hardly rising as he ran his tongue over each. But her slender body began to writhe, slow and snakelike, and his hands moved down her smooth skin, halted atop the almost bare little pubic mound, the sensation surprisingly erotic.

Her slender legs rose up, then fell away, and soft moaning sounds came from her, undulating, almost a half-whine. He turned his throbbing erectness atop her pubic mound, shifted, found the opened portal, and the undulating, moaning sounds continued on exactly the same level, growing neither louder nor softer. She was tight, soft smooth walls pressed against him, and a single gasp found its way through the soft moaning sound. Her hips lifted, her pelvis continued to writhe, and her hands were now hard against his back. Her tightness around him pressed, excited the flesh, and he fought back his desire to explode. He quickened his movements and she twisted her pelvis with him and the soft, undulating sounds continued to remain the same.

But as he grew quicker, harsher, fiercer, he heard the sudden gasped half-screams break into the wave-like moaning and he felt her grow tighter around him. "Aaaiiee, aaiieee, aiiieee," she cried as her pelvis quivered against him, and he felt himself carried with her. She sent out the short, almost staccato half-screams again and then again as her almost bare pubic mound pumped upward with him.

Then, with a long, sighing sound, she went limp and he lay atop her, staying inside her.

She made little murmuring sounds and her arms were around him, holding him in place until finally she let her arms fall away and he slid from her. She lay with her eyes closed, a slender child-woman figure with legs tightly together, her appearance a strange mixture of quiet properness and incipient sensuality. Her lovemaking had also been a strange mixture, he reflected. She had felt pleasure, responded, yet there had seemed more acceptance than ecstasy. Perhaps that, too, had roots in the distant past, the cultural and physical heritage of the role of the Pawnee woman.

He sat up, started to dress, and she opened her eyes and watched. She rose when he finished, slipped the deerskin dress on, and followed him to the Ovaro, an unmistakable air of smugness to her.

He turned her to face him, his hand on her shoulder. "You wanted it to happen. Why?"

"You took me from all the bluecoats," she said.

"I told you, your father sent me to do this."

"Because you are a great warrior. But he will kill you now. But I have honored your deed in my way," she said. "Now there will be no shame on him or on me."

"All nice and neat," Fargo grunted. "The Pawnee way of saving face. Get on the horse."

She pulled herself onto the Ovaro and he swung into the saddle behind her. Never look a gift horse in the mouth, he reminded himself. But she had confirmed his feelings about Red Buffalo.

Fargo moved downhill through the heavy tree cover. He had passed above and now behind the last line of lookouts, and he worked his way down to the Pawnee camp in a series of half-circles until he reached level terrain.

The camp lay but a hundred yards ahead of him and the first hint of dusk touched the sky when he rode in with the girl in front of him. He didn't hide his smile as he saw the Pawnee chief, outside near his tepee, turn at the murmur that rose from his braves. Red Buffalo stared at him, astonishment flooding his massive head. He quickly pulled his usual stoic composure around himself as Fargo halted in front of him. "I should have known you could find your way here alone," the Indian said.

Fargo nodded and let Moonglow slide from the Ovaro. She landed lightly on the ground and hurried to her father, put her forehead against his chest in a gesture that was gratitude, caring, and homage all rolled together. The Pawnee chief touched his hand to her head and she turned to stand beside him.

"I've kept my part of the bargain," Fargo said.

"You have," the Indian nodded.

"Now you keep yours."

The Pawnee nodded again and Fargo swung to the ground. "Take your people out of here," Red Buffalo said, and barked orders to some of his braves, who hurried away to cut the captives loose. Fargo followed and waited as the rawhide thongs were severed and he saw some of the woman sobbing in relief, the men with a mixture of surprise and gratitude in their drawn faces. Clarissa's sister ran to him, her eyes wide as she flung herself against him. A tall, thin man with a lined face stepped forward.

"This is real, you got them to let us go?" he asked, and Fargo nodded. "I'm Zed Bench, wagonmaster," the man added.

"Get your wagons. Get everybody back into them," Fargo said, and walked with the others, Ada clinging to him, to where the Conestogas waited.

He waited for everyone to climb into the wagons before he climbed into the saddle and drew up alongside Zed Bench in the first Conestoga.

"Follow me. No hurrying. Nice and slow," Fargo said, and put the pinto into a walk.

Red Buffalo stood outside his tepee, his braves lined up the length of the camp, each face more expressionless than the next. Fargo paused in front of the Indian chief and let his glance go to Moonglow. Her eyes held the hint of a satisfied smile and he glanced back to Red Buffalo.

"I chose well," the Pawnee said, and made no effort to hide the triumph in his voice.

"Seems that way," Fargo agreed. "Better than you think," he added, and enjoyed the moment's frown that touched the massive head. He moved on, the Conestogas creaking along behind him and moving even more slowly as they threaded their way through the thick forest terrain that led to the camp. Fargo guessed they had perhaps another hour's daylight left when they finally emerged from the dense trees and onto more open land. When dusk began to turn to night, he found a half-circle of trees ideal for camping and ordered the wagons to a halt.

He watched from the side as figures climbed down from the wagons, formed a circle, and Zed Bench led a prayer service. They turned to Fargo when it was finished.

"You must be some kind of miracle man, mister," Zed said.

"The name's Fargo. . . . Skye Fargo, and it was no miracle. More of an exchange too thorny to explain now. Truth is, I'm afraid you're not home-free."

"They're going to come at us again?" someone asked.

"I'm thinking that. But it won't be till sometime tomorrow," Fargo said. "I made some plans. If I guessed right, they might save all our hides."

The man nodded gravely and walked to where the others were beginning to bed down.

Fargo led the pinto some fifty yards away, found a low-branched hawthorn, and set his things out. He slept soundly, exhaustion demanding nothing less, and woke with the morning sun. Someone had made a small fire and put on coffee. He walked to the wagons and a woman handed him a tin mug of strong black brew.

It was obvious that Zed Bench had spoken to the others because coffee was taken in solemn silence, their joy at no longer being captives tempered by the specter of another attack.

When they were ready to roll, he led the way down into small, winding paths through the hills, some rising steeply to strain the horses as they pulled the heavy prairie schooners. His eyes swept the terrain on all sides, especially to their rear, but he saw no sign of any bronzed figures following. It was past the noon hour when he'd called a rest that he dismounted and scanned the hills that rose on both sides, a thick cover of black oak on one, an equally thick mantle of box elder on the other. Again, he saw nothing, but he suddenly felt the hairs on the back of his neck rise.

No imagination, he murmured to himself. He felt that sixth sense they called intuition that took over when neither sight nor sound nor smell delivered any message. It had come to him often enough not to push it away. They were there, he was certain, silent and invisible as wraiths, but they were there. They had caught up, probably moving in small clusters, perhaps not more than two or three together, filtering through the thick hill forests. He could feel them, but he decided to say nothing to the others. He wanted no sign of panic, no terror-filled faces casting anxious glances into the hills. It was important that the Pawnee remain smugly confident. He wanted them to see nothing that might hasten an attack. He still needed to buy time.

He climbed onto the pinto and waved the wagons forward. He stayed a hundred yards ahead for another hour, then dropped back fifty yards closer, then another twenty-five. He continued to sweep the hills with seemingly casual glances, as he had done all day, only there was nothing casual about them. But he still saw no signs of the silent forms he knew were in the trees. He peered ahead and spat into the wind. The spot where he had left Baker and the column was still a good half-hour away and he wiped the perspiration on the palms of his hands on his shirt.

Red Buffalo was leading his warriors, that was a certainty. It would be for him alone to decide when he had allowed enough time and distance to pass to honor the agreement as he saw it. Fargo allowed himself a grim smile. So far he had guessed correctly. The Pawnee chief wanted to be sure no one could accuse him of breaking his word. Or perhaps he simply wanted to satisfy his own conscience. Honor, even twisted by hate and destiny, was still an important thing.

White men weren't the only ones who could rationalize their misdeeds, Fargo realized, the thought of little comfort. Time was running out. In the distance, he could glimpse the hillside where he had left Baker and his men. It seemed just one more hillside, tree-covered and silent, and for a moment he had the terrible thought that perhaps Baker had decided to pull up stakes and go searching for him. But it was nerves that jabbed at him, he realized, and flung the thought aside. He slowed and came alongside Zed Bench.

"So far it seems we're doing right well," the man observed. "Maybe you were wrong about them coming after us."

"Maybe," Fargo said. "But just to be safe, if I yell run, you get these wagons rolling as fast as they can go. Understand?"

"Sure thing," Zed said.

"And if I yell take cover, you pull up and start shooting," Fargo said.

Zeb Bench nodded but threw him a sidelong glance. "You see something?"

"Not a thing," Fargo said, an honest answer. "Pass the word along," he said, and rode on a dozen paces ahead. He turned and rode back along the side of the wagon. Some of the children waved out at him as he wheeled and rode at the rear. Again, he scanned the hills on both sides as the Conestogas followed the narrow trail between them. His eyes narrowed as they peered into the distance. The trail widened and became a low plateau. He grimaced—it was the perfect spot for the Pawnee to strike. They could sweep down from the tree cover and onto the plateau. The hillside where he'd left the lieutenant rose up now at the end of the low plateau.

Fargo's eyes turned to the box elder and slowly scanned the hill, and suddenly he saw movement through the trees, a single horseman. He moved his eyes to the left and saw another. Three more rustled the low branches as they moved down. "Shit," he muttered, and cast a glance at the distant hillside. So near and suddenly so far. His eyes went to the opposite hill, where the black oak formed a protective screen, and now he saw the half-naked riders moving downhill.

They were still moving casually, still full of confidence. But time had run out, Fargo realized. His eyes went to the distant hillside. An ambush was out of the question now, the effective results of a hard first strike vanished. Baker would have to move out into the open for a pitched battle. But one bright spot still remained: the Pawnee Chief had his daughter. He'd do battle, but he'd have no reason to fight to extinction. He'd want his warriors with him to fight another day.

Fargo swore softly. Not if he could help it, he promised.

8

Fargo spurred the Ovaro forward and came abreast of Zed Bench in the first wagon. "Run," he shouted, saw Zeb look at him with a moment of fear and then snap the reins hard over the brace of horses. He let out a roar at the same time and the big Conestoga moved forward with surprising speed.

Fargo dropped back, wheeled, and saw the others take off after the lead wagon. He reined to a halt as he watched the Conestogas race away onto the low plateau, and then his eyes went to the two hills. He had only seconds to wait when the horde of near-naked riders poured from the trees on both sides, their short-legged ponies moving into a gallop.

He heard their war whoops and sought out the massive figure of Red Buffalo, but he was not leading the charge. He was hanging back, moving into position to see and to signal his warriors. He would be in the black oak to the right, Fargo was certain. It afforded the best line of sight.

Fargo swung the Ovaro around and raced after the wagons. The two bands of attackers had merged and were streaking after the Conestogas. Fargo reached the wagons, raced to the front, and threw a glance back and waved Zeb Bench on. He unholstered the Colt, took aim at two Pawnee coming close and outdistancing the others. He fired and one flew from his mount while the other peeled away.

He took aim at another Pawnee racing up, and the Indian pitched forward as he fell to the ground. But the main body of the attackers was drawing close.

"Take cover," Fargo shouted at Zeb Bench, and saw the man pull back on the reins and wheel the big Conestoga to a stop, the side facing the attacks. The other wagons did the same as they rolled to a stop, the front end of one overlapping the rear of the next. Those inside leapt to the ground, the men with rifles kneeling behind the wheels, the women and children taking cover beneath the wagons.

Fargo drew the big Sharps as he jumped from the Ovaro and flattened himself behind the wheels of Zeb Bench's wagon. He fired through the spaces between the spokes as the Pawnee attacked, and brought down two with his first volley.

Most of the Pawnee were using bows, their arrows thudding into the wagons and tearing through the canvas, but some had rifles. Fargo picked out one with a rifle and knocked the man sideways from his mount with a single shot. He took a moment to cast a glance down the plateau to the hillside. Nothing moved and he cursed and returned his attention to the Pawnee. They were circling now, and he flipped onto his back as he fired and took down another attacker. His next shot broke off a war whoop as it all but blew the Pawnee's head off. Cursing, he cast another quick glance down the plateau. Baker had to have heard the shots and the war whoops by now. Where the hell was he? Fargo swore and suddenly felt the shout gather in his throat. The hillside was erupting with blue-uniformed figures charging from the trees on their brown army mounts.

They came at a full gallop in two columns, and Fargo saw the Pawnee slow their attack and wheel in surprise. His eyes went to the hillside of black oak and he saw the massive figure on a gray pony raise his arm, a lance clutched in his fist. The braves wheeled again and raced to meet the charging cavalry. They outnumbered Baker's men, but Fargo saw the lieutenant spread the two columns into a long, single line as they charged, firing their rifles as they did. The first cluster of Pawnee went down while their shots and arrows missed most of the spaced-apart troopers. A second volley fired with military precision sent another cluster of Pawnee down, though three troopers fell from their mounts.

Fargo leapt onto the Ovaro and sent the horse around the back end of the wagons and raced toward the hillside of black oak, where he saw Red Buffalo watching, his arm with the lance still upraised.

He also saw the lieutenant send his troops into two columns again, one veering to the left, the other to the right so they could pour a cross fire into the Pawnee. He watched the Indians slow, wheel in alarm as more of their force went down, and his eyes went to Red Buffalo. The chief was pumping his arm up and down, and Fargo saw the braves peel away from the attack, racing off in two different directions as they did. But the Trailsman was into the oaks now, and he turned and began to cross the hill inside the forest.

He slowed as he neared the spot where he had seen Red Buffalo and leaned from the saddle to peer through the trees. But the Indian chief had moved and Fargo pressed forward cautiously. Below, the sounds of the cavalry rifles still echoed, but more sporadically. The lieutenant had his men chasing after the fleeing Pawnee. Fargo hoped he'd remember what happened the last time he engaged in headlong pursuit, and would call a halt in time. His eyes narrowed as he moved through the trees, searching ahead for the Pawnee chief. He moved between two thick-trunked oaks, the Sharps ready to fire, when he pulled to a halt as a small, slender figure looked up at him.

"Moonglow," he murmured in surprise. "He brought you along?"

"I wanted to come," she said.

He was frowning at her, surprise still holding him, his alertness compromised. He heard the swish of air behind him and twisted away, but the lance struck him in the back of his shoulder. He felt himself pitch forward over the horse's neck as pain exploded down the left side of his body. He hit the ground and knew he'd lost his grip on the rifle as flashing lights exploded in his head. He lay still, the light still flashing, and felt another sharp stab of pain. The world disappeared for a moment, or what seemed like a moment, and when his eyes came open again, he was on his back and he stared up at Red Buffalo's massive head. The tip of the lance touched his throat and he pressed his arm against his holster. It was empty.

The slender figure came into focus beside the Pawnee chief and he saw the Colt in her hand. The Pawnee pulled the tip of the lance back. "Get up," he commanded, and Fargo pushed to his feet and felt a moment of dizziness as the pain shot through his left shoulder blade.

Moonglow handed her father the Colt and stepped into the trees to emerge leading a heavyset pony and a tan-and-white horse, almost a Tobiano but not quite. She effortlessly pulled herself onto the horse, the deerskin dress rising to reveal the slender, shapely legs that had been around his hips. Red Buffalo mounted the other pony and gestured to the Ovaro.

Using his right arm only, Fargo pulled himself

onto the pinto and again felt the wave of dizziness shoot through him. Red Buffalo swung in a few paces behind him and he felt the lance prod him in the back as Moonglow rode ahead. "Follow her," the Pawnee said, and emphasized his words by pushing the lance harder into Fargo's back.

"Why not kill me here?" Fargo asked.

"Moonglow said she would like you as a slave," the chief answered.

"A great warrior does not deserve that."

"A great warrior will not allow that," Red Buffalo said. "He will turn and attack and be killed."

Fargo shot a grim glance back at the Pawnee. "Convenient. I guess I'm not that great a warrior," he said.

Red Buffalo uttered a sound that somehow managed to combine caution and contempt.

The girl stayed in the trees, led the way higher and along a narrow ridge.

Lieutenant Baker would send a patrol scouring the nearby terrain for him, Fargo knew, and eventually begin the ride back to the stockade. The wagons would follow and Clarissa would have emerged to join her sister and the others by now. There had been casualties, of course, but for the most part, they had survived. He had accomplished what he'd set out to do, Fargo told himself, and wondered if the old martyrs had trouble feeling satisfaction and pride as they faced death.

It was dusk when Moonglow led the way into the Pawnee camp and Red Buffalo removed the lance from his back. Two braves pulled him from the Ovaro and tied his wrists with rawhide thongs. They took him to a small tepee at the far end of the camp, and a dozen old squaws prodded and poked at him as he was led past.

Moonglow held the tent flap open as he was

pushed inside, and a small fire of twigs in a hollowed-out circle of earth gave a soft light. His ankles were bound and he was thrown to the ground, and another, longer length of rawhide bound his legs to a heavy piece of log. The braves left and he stared up at the Indian girl as he lay on his back.

"Why?" he asked. "You wanted me to take you. You honored my deed for yourself and for your father. Why this?"

"That was done. It is past, just as one day ends and another begins," she said. "I will get the medicine man for your wound." She left on silent steps.

Fargo lay in the small tepee, tried to move his legs, and found the heavy log allowed him only a fraction of an inch. His shoulder sent shafts of pain through him at the effort, and he lay back as his thoughts raced. Moonglow had been somewhat of a puzzle, and now she was an enigma. But if he could use her to buy time, he'd find a way to free himself. His thoughts broke off as she returned with two braves and an old man who carried various pouches of hide and cloth. The two braves sat him up as they stripped off his shirt and then turned him on his side and he winced in pain.

He lay still and felt the old man's hands on him, surprisingly gentle, wiping blood from the wound into his shoulder blade. His eyes could see only Moonglow as she watched, and he found himself staring at the contained, stoic beauty of her. He felt powder being sprinkled onto the wound, flesh contracting at the touch of it, then more powder applied. He heard the rattle of beads being shaken inside a shell, and he was turned on his back and saw the shaman holding the medicine bundle over him. The old man chanted in a singsong voice, words Fargo could not decipher, and then stopped as suddenly as he had begun. He turned and left with the two braves and Moonglow followed with a glance back at Fargo.

The Trailsman drew a deep sigh and lay still. He pushed aside making plans. Everything was too uncertain for that. But he decided that the Indian girl was his only hope. For reasons he couldn't define yet, she wanted him alive, at least for a while. Perhaps longer, perhaps not. She was indeed an enigma, and he closed his eyes and let himself catnap.

The night had grown deeper when he came awake again. He carefully moved his shoulder. The pain was still there, but nothing like what it had been. The shaman's powder was effective, he reckoned, and moved his shoulder again, as much as his bonds would let him. The pain was but a dull ache now. He was not so much surprised as impressed by the astounding power of ancient remedies. He was staring at the roof of the tepee when the slender form entered.

Moonglow halted before him, dropped to her knees, and her black eyes searched his face. "Your shoulder is better," she said.

"Yes. How did you know," he asked in some surprise.

"There is no pain in your eyes now. The shaman's powder is powerful. It is made of birch bark and wolfsbane."

He peered at her and she did not look away. "You did not answer my question before. Why?" he asked.

"My father wanted to kill you," she said. "I told him it would be a special thing for a chief's daughter to have a great warrior as her slave."

"Do you really want that?"

"Yes," she said, and she leaned forward, whisked the deerskin dress off, and knelt in her child-woman provocative loveliness before him. Her hands pulled his gun belt off, pulled open his trouser buttons, and pushed trousers and underdrawers down to his ankles. She let her eyes linger on him and he saw her lips part as tiny, short breaths escaped them. She took her hands and began to rub them down his body, starting at his face, moving to his chest, down across the muscled hardness of his abdomen, and finally down further. He felt himself responding as she began, and when she reached his groin, he was rising, throbbing, and he swallowed away the dryness in his mouth.

She touched him exploringly, gently pulled and caressed, obviously taken with her discoveries. She half-rose and lay over him, stretched her body to its fullest, and pressed the almost bare pubic mound over his throbbing warmth. He felt her quiet excitement as she loved slowly up and down along his body. Her breath now came in a long, hissing sound. The thought raced across his mind.

"No, I can't, not like this," he said, and she halted, her eyes searching his face. "Not with my legs tied."

She hesitated for a moment and then lifted herself from him, went to the deerskin dress, and drew a knife from an inside pouch. She cut the thongs that bound his legs to the log and then those that tied his ankles together.

"My arms," he said, but she shook her head and tossed the knife aside as she lay down over him again. Another thought slid through his mind, prodded at him, and he brought one leg up and put it around her back. "Is this why you want me as your slave?" he asked.

"It will be one of your duties," she said. "When I want you." She tried to keep her voice filled with regal composure, but he detected something more and another thought exploded inside him.

"When you wanted me in the mountains, was that the first time for you?"

"Yes," she said, and he held the smile inside him. He'd always heard it was true and this was a confirmation—they never forget the first time. If it was good, they remembered it with warm fondness. If it was bad, they remembered it with distaste. But they always remembered. And at the time, it was to be savored, held tight, preserved. Moonglow had found her way to preserve it, to relive whenever she wanted. But he also knew something more. In time she would tire of him. She would want to try others, new experiences, great warriors of her own people. She was a creature of strong-willed curiosity. It was inevitable.

Then she would reduce him to memory, and that could only be done one way. She would not flinch at that. She was a chief's daughter and anything she did was right. But his thoughts slid away as he felt his groin surge and heard his groan of pleasure as her pubic mound slid back and forth across him, exciting, stimulating, her wanting warmth beyond denying. She took her hands, clasped them on his hips, and rolled him atop her. Her slender legs fell apart and she pushed upward. Not imploring, her demanding hands dug into his buttocks as she pressed him forward. He wanted to make his move now, but his loins vetoed the thought. He'd give her another moment to remember. Not that she especially deserved it, he decided as he moved his hips, found her opened portal, and plunged deeply.

She uttered a small gasped sound and she was still tight around him. This time he moved quickly, thrusting hard, sliding back, pushing deep again. Her tiny, undulating moans began, continued as he stayed with her, quickening his movements until there were no thoughts of anything but the pleasures of the flesh. It was awkward with his hands tied behind his back and the dull throb of his shoulder irritated. But the supremacy of the senses pushed aside everything else and suddenly the undulating soft moans stopped. Her warmth tightened around him and she quivered against him until finally she fell back, a short gasp exploding from her lips.

He drew from her, fell to his side against her, and realized there had been fury as well as pleasure in his taking of her. She was as manipulatively cunning as her father, in her own way. Given time, she'd be as ruthless, Fargo was convinced. He lay still alongside her and let his body restore itself until she moved and sat up. She looked down at him and her small smile was made of satisfied smugness. He watched her move toward the deerskin dress, and he lay with one leg straight, the other raised and bent at the knee.

"Come back," he called softly, and she halted to look at him. "There is more to show you," he murmured invitingly. "Come back."

She crawled toward him on her hands and knees, and he waited, tensed his thigh and calf muscles, and when she was within range, snapped his knee upward. The blow smashed into the point of her chin and she pitched forward unconscious.

Fargo spun, rolled to where she had flung the knife, and turned onto his back to pick the blade up. The thongs allowed enough give so he could work the blade against them with quick, sharp strokes. They parted just as Moonglow moaned. He leapt to his feet, pulled on his clothes, and paused to look at her. She stirred and her eyelids fluttered. He lifted her to a sitting position and brought a quick blow to her chin and let her fall back. "Sorry, honey. All's fair in love and war," he muttered. "Old white man's expression."

146

He stepped to the tent flap and knelt as he peered out. The camp was asleep and he crept from the tepee on silent steps, scanned the edge of the camp, and spotted the Ovaro tied with the other Indian ponies. He made his way around the edges of the camp, sleeping figures dotting the ground, until he reached the horses and slipped the Ovaro's reins from the long rawhide tether. He led the horse from the camp, one soft step at a time. His eyes scanned the tepees and the figures of those who slept on the ground outside. No one moved and yet he felt uneasy, as though he were being watched.

The feeling persisted as he paused every few yards to scan the camp again. But nothing moved, and he went on, rounded the far end where the wooden council hut stood, made his way back along the other side, and headed into the thicket-dark forest that would lead him to safety. He didn't mount the Ovaro till he'd gone another fifty yards into the woods. Then he put the horse into a canter as he saw the first tint of the new day touch the sky. He had gone perhaps another half-mile when he caught the unmistakable sound of the soft thud of unshod hooves coming after him. He increased his speed and then slowed and listened again. The hoofbeats were closer, the horse at a gallop.

Only one horse, he noted as he turned and backed the Ovaro into a thicket. The lone figure came into sight as the new dawn filtered through the trees, and he saw the massive head at once, the lance in the man's hand.

Red Buffalo reined to a hard stop as he saw the Ovaro's tracks end. He slid from the pony, stayed behind it, and turned the horse in a slow circle as he scanned the trees. He halted as he faced the thicket and Fargo edged the Ovaro forward until he halted only a few yards from the Pawnee chief.

"It was you who watched me leave the camp," he said, and the Indian nodded.

"I told my daughter to let me finish you. She refused. She said she could deal with you," the chief said. "I saw her bring the shaman to you and then go back later herself. I wanted to believe she could deal with you and keep you as a slave. I waited and finally I saw you come from the tepee alone. I watched you circle the camp and leave and went to the tepee to see to Moonglow."

"When you found she was alive, you came after me," Fargo said, and the chief made no reply. None was needed. The next question on the tip of Fargo's tongue was unneeded also, he realized.

Red Buffalo had come after him alone, instead of waking his warriors to give chase. Of course, Fargo realized. He had to come alone. To waken the others would reveal Moonglow's foolish craving for this intruder, and her failure. It would cast dishonor upon her and himself. He had indulged her when he should have insisted on obedience. He had no choice but to come alone.

"You will die," the Pawnee said, snapping off Fargo's thoughts.

Fargo's lips tightened. He considered wheeling the Ovaro and racing away while the Indian was beside his horse. But he knew the lance would go through his back before he could get far enough away. Red Buffalo stepped out from behind his pony and Fargo's quick glance showed him that the forest didn't allow enough room for him to charge the Ovaro at him with sufficient speed or maneuverability. He swore softly as he swung to the ground. It was his turn to have no choice.

The Indian moved toward him, the lance thrust out straight. With steps that were surprisingly quick, he executed what seemed almost a little dance as he feinted with his feet and then lunged forward with the lance. Fargo twisted away, backed, kept his shoulders squared away, and faced the Indian. Red Buffalo moved forward again, little quick thrusting lunges with the lance, and now it was Fargo who did a little dance as he barely avoided the point of the weapon. Suddenly, taking him by complete surprise, the Indian twirled the lance, almost as a drum major twirls a baton, and Fargo stayed in a half-crouch, unsure of which way to move.

With practiced deftness, Red Buffalo stopped twirling the lance and lashed out in a flat arc with it, using it more as a club. Fargo tried to twist away, but the lance caught him along the side of the head and he went down on one knee. He glimpsed the Indian driving the lance point at him, and he let himself fall backward, the weapon grazing his face. But he kicked one foot out and felt the blow catch the Pawnee chief in the kneecap. With a grunt of pain, the Indian went down and Fargo saw his Colt wedged in the waistband of the chief's breechclout. He dived headlong into the Indian, bowled him over as he yanked the Colt from the waistband.

Red Buffalo had rolled and regained his feet, the lance in his hand. He charged forward, his massive head lowered, not unlike a buffalo's charge, Fargo thought as he pulled the trigger of the Colt. The click of the hammer on an empty chamber hit his ears as though it were an explosion.

He flung himself sideways in a rolling dive as the lance tore through the collar of his shirt, came up, fired again and again, and each time there was only the sound of an empty chamber. The Pawnee was charging again, lance held in front of him, and Fargo held his ground another ten seconds and then flung the Colt into the massive face. It smashed into Red Buffalo's nose at the bridge, and Fargo saw the spurt of red erupt as the Indian's charge halted. He stepped in, threw a long, looping left that landed on the Pawnee's jaw, followed with a pile driver right to the same place. Red Buffalo staggered back, the lance dropping low, and Fargo seized the long pole with both hands, dug heels into the ground, and whirled the Pawnee in a circle.

He let go and the Indian flew against a tree with a bone-shaking crash. The lance fell from his hand and Fargo dived for it, got his hands on it, and rolled away from a vicious kick. He turned on his back and saw the Pawnee diving onto him with both hands outstretched. He kicked himself back six inches and managed to bring the lance around as the Indian landed on him. He felt the shuddering impact through his arms and shoulders and saw the Pawnee chief's eyes all but bulge out of their sockets as he impaled himself on the lance. A guttural sound fell from his lips, then a gusher of red as he toppled sideways, and Fargo saw the point of the lance protruding from his back.

The Trailsman rose to his feet, retrieved the Colt, and loaded it with the cartridges from his gun belt. Others would come searching for their chief. They'd find him and take him back. But Red Buffalo's reign was over. It would take time to choose a new chief and he would have to take more time to make his own decisions. Things would quiet down for a while, at least, and time was always a blessing. Fargo let a long sigh draw from deep inside him as he climbed onto the Ovaro and began the long ride back. Moonglow would not be remembering him with such fondness. He smiled and took pleasure in that.

But he turned his thoughts to things still to be done. Loose ends. First was Duvall. He'd be almost three days later than he'd expected returning to the man, but he was confident the major would still be there. He had tied the bonds well.

The day had slid into afternoon as he neared the place where he'd left the man. Baker had returned everyone to the stockade, probably giving up hope for him. Except for Clarissa. She'd keep believing. He walked the Ovaro slowly through the smooth sumac as he peered ahead to find the tree with Duvall tied to it.

But he spotted no uniformed figure and a furrow dug into his forehead as he halted before a tall tree. This had been the tree, he muttered. He was certain of it. He dismounted and went to the tree and saw the marks of the lariat where it had pressed into the bark. He knelt down and found the small pieces of lariat amid the leaves, pieces that had been cut. He rose and started to rest one hand on his gun when a shot exploded and he felt the searing pain of the bullet as it grazed his temple. He fell, the forest swimming away. He knew he lay facedown on the ground, the odor of moss and leaves in his nostrils. But the world was still a curtained place. Finally he felt the curtain lift. He shook his head, felt a trickle of blood down the side of his face, warm stickiness, and the world took shape again. He rose and saw Duvall waiting with an old rim-fire Remington .44 in his hand.

"Been waiting for you to come back, you rotten bastard," the major said. "Surprised, aren't you?"

"I am." Fargo nodded and winced at the pain in his temple.

"I got lucky. A trapper came along and set me loose. I bought this gun and some food from him and settled down and waited. You took longer than I expected, but I knew you'd be coming back," Duval said, a snarling smile on his face. "Now I'm going to put you in front of a firing squad. Baker, too."

"You left an order for Baker. All he did was follow it," Fargo protested.

"He should've known better," Duvall said.

"You can't put him in front of a firing squad for that."

"Then I'll have him cashiered from the service," the major snapped. "But you go before a firing squad. I could've killed you just now, but your friend Leeds might ask questions. This way it'll all be proper, with charges drawn up and punishment according to regulations."

"Red Buffalo is dead. His captives were brought out alive. Your troop had some casualties, but not that many. A bloodbath was prevented. Doesn't that mean anything to you?" Fargo questioned.

"It means I didn't wipe them all out and I won't get the credit for it," Duvall said. "It means you got in my way, and you're going to pay for it."

Fargo stared at the man. Duvall had refused to listen to reason before. He was going to do the same now. Obsession and reason don't go together, he reminded himself. "You're a goddamn lunatic," Fargo said. "You shouldn't ever wear that uniform."

"But I'm going to be wearing it and you'll wear a pine box," Duvall said, and his smile was evil triumph. "Drop the gun, nice and easy," the major said.

Fargo obeyed and stepped back as the man picked up the Colt. Duvall slapped his thigh and the brown army mount stepped from the trees. He climbed onto the horse and motioned for Fargo to mount the Ovaro. Duvall swung in behind him. The man wanted a firing squad, but he wouldn't hesitate to do the job himself if he had to, Fargo realized as he walked the horse slowly through the sumac.

They left the sumac and rode into more open land. He could feel Duvall directly behind him, the revolver aimed at the small of his back. He had to find a way to make the man change his position, he thought as his gaze swept the terrain. But they rode another hour and he hadn't found a place or a way, and he knew there was not much more than another hour's ride to the stockade. The narrow path wandered downward and Fargo's eyes sharpened as he saw a thick stand of hawthorn that bordered the path. Dense box elder took over just behind the hawthorn, he saw, with plenty of thick brush mixed in.

His hands held tightly together, he gave a quick, sharp pull on one rein and then drew back with the other. The Ovaro gave a sudden half-step in response. He paused, did it again, and the horse gave another half-step. Hardly moving his hands, keeping his arms perfectly still, Fargo did the same thing, and once again the Ovaro seemed to limp.

"What the hell's going on?" Duvall snapped as Fargo reined up.

"He's gone lame. Probably has a rock stuck in the frog," Fargo said, and Duvall drew up alongside him. "He can't go on this way. I'll take a look and get it out."

"Go on," Duvall grunted, and kept the gun trained on him as he swung from the Ovaro.

Fargo walked to the horse's left forefoot, picked it up, and peered at it.

Duvall was on the other side of the Ovaro. His shot would be at a bad angle. "Well?" Duvall growled.

"I see it," Fargo said. "Small pebble." He lifted the horse's hoof a fraction higher, shot a glance at Duvall, and saw that the man had relaxed a fraction. Fargo, twisting his body as he dived, flung himself into the hawthorn with explosive speed. Duvall's shot, delayed by surprise, was wild when it came. His second shot was fired too quickly, and was equally wild. But Fargo was running through the thick brush as the major brought his horse around and sent the mount crashing through the shrubbery.

Fargo halted and dropped down in the heavy undergrowth beneath the box elder, holding his breath in as Duvall slowed and passed by less than a dozen feet from him. He saw the major halt, listen, peer into the thick brush and the heavy tree cover. Fargo's hand moved along the ground and he touched a small rock, flat on both sides, the kind little boys love to send skimming across a pond.

With a quick flip of his wrist, he sent the stone skimming through the air to smash against a tree trunk in front of Duvall. The man whirled and fired and saw his shot bury itself in the gray-brown bark. Fargo heard Duvall's curse as the major slowly turned his horse in a circle. When the major's back was to him, Fargo exploded into a half-dive, half-run, and plunged into another, deeper thicket of brush.

Duvall lost precious seconds as he whirled his horse around and fired off two shots. That emptied the trapper's Remington, but he saw that Duvall was aware of that, too, as he pushed the gun into his waist and brought out the Colt.

He edged his horse slowly forward, some ten yards to the left of where Fargo lay, paused, and again turned in a slow circle as he scanned the brush. Fargo's hand slid along the ground and found another flat stone perfect for skimming. He moved his hand farther and came upon another. The forest floor was filled with the flat stones, probably chips from an underlying bed of rock. The first stone was small and he threw it to his right with the same quick motion he had the other. It sailed higher than the other, struck a branch, and Duvall fired two shots in the direction of the sound as he peered into the tree.

His luck wouldn't hold for Duvall to empty the Colt, Fargo realized. The man would hold back fire or get a bead on where the stones were coming from. Fargo's hand touched another flat stone, larger and heavier than the others, yet still perfectly shaped for skimming. He drew it into his hand as he watched Duvall peer into the forest, again slowly turning the horse.

He had to risk it, Fargo decided. If he missed, he'd be in real trouble. But if he didn't miss, he'd have perhaps his one last chance. He waited, shifted his arm, the large flat stone held in the palm of his hand with two fingers to guide the throw resting over and under it. Duvall's face was sideways in front of him, a perfect profile. Fargo fired the stone, saw it sail through the air in its flat trajectory and smash full-force into Duvall's temple. The man gave a curse of pain as he fell sideways from the horse. Fargo was racing forward before the major hit the ground.

Duvall, still dazed, lay on his side on the ground, but the Colt was in his hand as Fargo raced around the back of the horse. He kicked out with his right foot and sent the gun flying from the major's hand. He followed it with a running dive, clasped his fingers around the butt, and rolled as he got a proper grip on the gun. Duvall had recovered from his moment of pain and daze, and Fargo saw the man charging at him, an army-issue hunting knife in his hand. The Colt barked once and Duvall shuddered as he stumbled, took another step as his chest erupted in red, and pitch onto his face.

Fargo rose to his feet, holstered the Colt, and stared down at the still form for a long moment. He wanted to feel sorry for the man and realized he couldn't do it. He dragged him to his horse, lifted him facedown across the saddle, and walked back to the Ovaro. He rode the rest of the way without hurrying.

The stockade finally came into sight. The Conestoga wagons were lined up at the perimeter of the tents, and as he came abreast of the first tent, he saw the tall, strong figure race out. He leaned from the saddle as Clarissa threw her arms around his neck.

"Oh, God, oh, God. I never stopped hoping," she murmured.

"I knew you wouldn't," he said. "Throw some things together. I'll be back."

She nodded, drew her arms from around his neck, and he moved on into the stockade. He saw the troopers in the yard move toward him as he rode in.

Lieutenant Baker came from the office. "By God, we'd given you up for lost, Fargo," he said. "We searched for you for a day."

"I'm hard to lose," Fargo said. "Red Buffalo's dead. You can tell the people they can go back to their homes. Things will simmer down—for a while, at least."

Baker looked at the limp figure draped across the saddle. "What happened?"

"Accident. He had his gun out, stumbled, and shot himself," Fargo said.

The lieutenant looked at the dried blood alongside the big man's face. "That's a nasty wound you have there," he said. "Go see the company doctor. He'll clean it up for you."

"Much obliged," Fargo said, and Baker snapped commands at two of the men, who led Duvall's horse away. The lieutenant walked with Fargo to where the small red cross was tacked to a door.

"What happens now, Fargo?" Baker asked.

"I'll call on General Leeds in time. I'll tell him what happened. You'll be in command till they send a replacement for the major," Fargo said.

Baker offered a wry smile. "I was sort of hoping I could take over," he said. "But I know the army. They want rank and age in a command post."

"I'll remind them that Duvall had both of those things," Fargo said, and Baker's grin broadened.

"Thanks," he said, and left with a grateful handshake.

When Fargo finished with the company doctor, he walked from the stockade and saw some of the tents had already come down. Clarissa appeared, her filly behind her, a small leather sack hanging from the saddle horn.

"Ada's going to take my place for a while," she said. "Where are we going?"

"To a birthday party first," Fargo said. "That's what I started out to do, and by God I'm going to do it. I'll be late, but I'm going anyway."

"Good. I love birthday parties," Clarissa said, and climbed onto the filly and rode beside him as he headed southeast.

The night came swiftly and he bedded down on a high ridge that let the moonlight lay down its pale light. Clarissa's statuesque beauty took on a softer mantle, her deep-cupped breasts beautifully pale. She made love to him with a surging desire that carried the world away. When they finished, she lay with her breasts half over his chest.

"Every night," she murmured. "Every night."

"We'll be at Agatha's tomorrow night," he told her.

"All right. Every night after that," she said, curled into his arms, and slept in minutes.

He let the morning sun rise high past the dawn before he stirred and woke. Clarissa sat up, looking improperly awake, and he enjoyed watching the sway of her lovely breasts as she dressed. He found a stream nearby where they washed and an arbor of wild cherries for breakfast. He set a leisurely pace as they rode, his body still drained from the last few days, and the warm sun was enervating.

A little past noon he called a halt, found a shade tree, and decided to nap. A hillside stretched down to a field of brilliant red butterfly weed below.

"I'm going down to the flowers," Clarissa said, and he nodded, his hat pulled over his face. He listened to her make her way down the hillside and was surprised when, only a few minutes later, he heard her climbing back.

He was sitting up when she reached him and saw the dismay wreathing her face. "A man and woman down below the butterfly weed. They're going to be hung," she said.

Fargo rose to his feet. "You're sure of that?"

"They're stringing the rope over the branch of an oak."

"Who's they?" Fargo asked as he swung onto the Ovaro.

"Four men," Clarissa said. "Leastwise that's all I saw."

"Maybe we'd best have a look. You stay back," he said as he carefully guided the pinto down the steep hillside, through the scarlet butterfly weed, and slowed behind a rock that let him see to where an oak rose in lone splendor against a series of tall rocks.

Clarissa had been very right, he saw: a rope strung over a stout branch of the oak and a man and woman beneath it. The man was slight of build, a bland face with thinning hair, and the woman a frizzled blonde, moderately pretty. Four men faced the couple and Fargo felt the frown slide over his brow. Four men, something familiar about them. He edged the Ovaro closer and saw one of the men put the loop around the girl's neck.

"Ladies first," the man said, and the other three laughed.

"No, no," the small man shouted. "Leave her alone." He received a blow to the stomach that sent him to his knees, and the blonde was dragged to the tree.

Fargo slid from the Ovaro and took the big Sharps from the saddle case. He moved forward in quick, silent strides as his eyes swept the four hangmen again.

"I'll be damned," he muttered. "I'll be god-damned." The four had changed from being faintly familiar to very much so. They were the four that had ridden with Marilyn Evans. He darted forward, halted, raised the rifle, and fired at the one who had begun to yank the girl up by the neck. The man screamed as he clutched at his kneecap and fell to the ground.

Fargo stepped into the open as the other three spun in surprise. "Don't do anything stupid," he said. "Drop your guns." Two of the men obeyed, but the third one tried to draw and the big Sharps barked again. He fell, clutching at his side as his gun flew into the air.

The blonde had flung the noose from around her neck and run to the bland-faced man as Fargo allowed a wry smile to stay on his face. "You must be Sam Evans and Cindy, the famous runaways," he said.

Astonishment flooded the man's bland face. "Yes, but how did you know? Who are you?" he asked nervously.

"Name's Fargo. Your wife tried to get me to hunt

you down. I see these four clowns succeeded," Fargo said.

"Only by accident. Cindy and I hid from all the Indian activity. We'd have been far gone otherwise. They came onto us when we started to move again," Sam Evans said.

"Where's the sentimental Marilyn?" Fargo asked.

The shot was his answer, and it sent a spray of dirt up at his feet.

"Right here," the voice came from behind one of the rocks. "Drop the rifle or the next one goes into your belly."

Fargo cursed as he let the rifle drop to the ground. Marilyn Evans stepped from behind the rock, a big old plains Hawkens in her hands. "Bastard," she spit at him.

"Bitch," he returned. "Why were you hiding behind the rock? Can't stand to see people hung?"

"I've learned to be careful. Never be sure. You taught me that, Fargo," she said. "Always have a hole card."

The rifle shot exploded and Marilyn Evans screamed in pain as her gun flew out of her grip and she bent over clutching her hand.

"That's right, lady," Fargo heard Clarissa say as she stepped into the open, the rifle in her hands. He bent down and scooped up the Sharps as Marilyn turned back, her right hand pressed against her Levi's to stanch the bleeding.

"Hunting down a runaway husband's one thing. Hanging him and his girlfriend is another," Fargo said. "That's what you figured to do all the time, wasn't it? After I found them for you?"

"Go to hell," Marilyn snapped.

"Just out of curiosity, how'd you get the general to let you go?" he asked.

"He let me send a messenger to Plainsville and the sheriff came and testified for me. The general held us as long as he could, and then he had to release us."

Fargo turned to Sam Evans. "Take their guns and their horses, Sam. Ride out of here and keep riding."

"You can't do that. You have wounded people here. We're out in the middle of nowhere," Marilyn shouted.

"Crawl. Limp. Walk. You'll find your way to someplace," Fargo said.

"You bastard," Marilyn Evans spit at him again.

"I saw what you tried to do here, honey," Fargo said. "You ever go after Sam again and I'll blow the whistle. You can count on it." He turned to Sam Evans and the little blonde. "Go on. What are you waiting for?" he said, and the man hurried to the horses, his girlfriend with him. The Trailsman watched them until they disappeared into the distance, then he motioned to Clarissa and started to walk away with her.

"You can't do this. I have money. I'll pay you to get us to a town," Marilyn Evans shouted.

"Sorry. Remember that birthday party? I'm still going to it," he said, paused, and enjoyed the fury that contorted her face. He walked back to the Ovaro and Clarissa swung onto the filly. A quick glance back showed him the limping, crawling, walking figures beginning to move. "Let's ride," he said to Clarissa, and sent the pinto into a gallop.

"You want to tell me what that was all about?" she asked.

"A loose end," he said. He told her of how Marilyn had hired him and what had followed. He left out only a few parts. Discretion was still the better part of valor.

They reached a frame house standing all by itself on the plain, stable and barn a dozen yards away, as dusk began to descend.

Agatha's daughter, Amy, met him at the door with a giant embrace.

"How late am I?" he asked.

"Her birthday was last week," the woman said. "But you're here, and that's enough for another birthday party."

He went into the house, Clarissa beside him, and stared at Agatha Benson as she focused on him and her lips parted in a smile that held tears in it. She had aged, yet not so much that she'd changed terribly. In truth, she looked like a woman at least twenty-five years younger. "Better late than never, Agatha," Fargo said as he leaned down and embraced her.

"That's right, Fargo," the old woman said. "You're here. That's what matters. You made it."

"You made it, Agatha," he said.

"I'll be expecting you next year," she said, and Fargo nodded and found Clarissa's hand in his. Amy's husband and their sons came in from the barn and the evening went quickly with old stories and old memories. Agatha stayed up as long as everyone else.

"They'll put you in the guest room," he told Clarissa later. "These are proper folks."

"Of course," she said, squeezed his hand, and the evening came to an end.

They left after breakfast in the morning and Fargo rode into a long, low, lush valley, his silence made of many things.

"What are you thinking?" Clarissa asked.

"I'm thinking I never had such a hard time getting to a birthday party," he said.

"Any more loose ends?"

"No more."

"Wrong," she answered, and he frowned at her. "I'm going to be the loosest end you ever met," she said, pulled under a low-branched ironwood, and swung to the ground. She was unbuttoning her blouse as he came down beside her.

"I do believe you're right," Fargo said happily.

LOOKING FORWARD!
The following is the opening
section from the next novel in the exciting
Trailsman series from Signet:

THE TRAILSMAN #109
LONE STAR LIGHTNING

Summer 1860, in west Texas, below Pecos,
where outlaws rode in dust devils
to plunder, rape, and kill,
until one day at sundown. . . .

The big man astride the magnificent black-and-white
Ovaro rode slowly through low-growing greasewood
that dominated the flat landscape. Not unlike a
black and foreboding sea, the individual sun-dried
clumps stretched monotonously from horizon to horizon. Stunted mesquite, charred black by the fiery
sun, and yucca dotted the dark prairie.

Directly overhead blazed an angry sun as white as
the sky in which it hung. It beat down unmercifully
on the rider and the sunbaked, desolate terrain.

White alkaline dust covered the man and his horse.
Shortly after sunrise he had pulled his neckerchief
up to just below his lake-blue eyes. It had done
precious little good. The choking dust had quickly
plugged his ears and nostrils. A thin layer covered
his parched lips, which he refused to lick.

A bone-dry canteen hung from his saddle horn.

He had dripped the last few drops of the tepid water onto the pinto's tongue at sundown the previous day. Earlier he had seen six longhorns foraging for stubbled prairie grass, so he knew water was nearby. An hour passed before he spotted a rather large but shallow depression. He went to it and found the water hole's bottom arid, baked brick-hard. He dug his stiletto between a crack and probed for moisture. Finding none, he mounted up and rode on.

Like the powerful stallion's, the big man's head also drooped. Both sought a measure of relief from the blistering sun. The only sounds came from the tiresome plodding of the horse's hooves. They went unheard by the napping rider.

Dust devils pirouetted among dry Russian thistle, cacti, and the seemingly endless greasewood. A white trail of dust traced their dizzy course.

The prairie and all on it shimmered in heat waves rising off the scorched and cracked earth. One of the whirlwinds danced out of the rippling waves of heat, uprooted a parched Russian thistle, and tumbled the large ball-like growth into the Ovaro. The stallion snorted a protest at the rough annoyance and deftly hopped his hind legs over it.

Waving the swirling white dust out of his face, Skye Fargo glanced at the dust devil skipping off into the heat waves on his left. Far beyond the playful whirlwind, highly magnified by the ripple effect of the heat waves, loomed a two-story house, barns, and a bunkhouse.

Fargo's first thought was of water. He and the thirsty pinto desperately needed it. He turned toward the ranch house. A lone turkey vulture circling lazily overhead swooped down and alit in front of the house. The meat-eating scavenger's presence meant only one thing: death.

Coming closer, Fargo saw many buzzards huddled on the front steps and at the bunkhouse. The scavengers were stripping rotted flesh off the bones of a man's body lying askew on the steps. The vultures craned to watch Fargo dismount; then, as though unconcerned over having their meal interrupted, they hopped onto the porch rail.

Going up the steps, Fargo noted the shotgun lying on the bones of the man's right hand, and the three black crusted bloodstained bullet holes in the front of his shirt. The vultures dropped from their perches and returned immediately to the man's remains when Fargo opened the screen door.

The stench inside the baking-hot room was overpowering. He jerked his neckerchief up over his nose. It did little good. He glanced around the room. A narrow staircase led up to the second floor. A woman's body lay on a daybed. Her dress had been ripped in two down the front. It went without saying she'd been sexually violated before her throat was slashed. The broiling heat had rolled the edges of the wide, deep cut inside out. She hadn't gone down without putting up a fight. Overturned chairs in the otherwise tidy room showed her path of flight. Fargo stepped into the kitchen.

He found her table set for four. The meal was on the stove, cooking when interrupted by the intruder. The food in the scorched pots was unrecognizable. He opened the oven door and saw the blackened remains of a hen that had been baked to a crisp. The hen meant she had been preparing a Sunday supper. He looked at a pailful of drinking water setting on the draining board. Two canteens hung from a peg above the pail. Fargo guzzled from the water bucket. Then he took the canteens and the rest of the water to his horse.

After whetting the Ovaro's thirst, he went back inside and looked up the stairwell. Pulling the neckerchief up over his nose again, Fargo took three strides to reach the top landing. Three doors opened onto as many bedrooms.

He found nobody in the first and presumed it was the man's and his wife's. On the floor in the second room he found the body of a boy that he guessed might have seen his tenth birthday. The youngster's hand still gripped one corner of the sheet he'd pulled from the bed. Flies swarmed over what was left of the lad's face, chewed away from a shotgun blast held close. Fargo shook his head and went to the third door.

A grizzly scene, more hideous than any of the others, greeted him. A girl—by the length of her bloated, nude body Fargo reckoned she was fourteen, certainly not over sixteen—lay with her legs parted wide on the blood-soaked bed. A shotgun blast from close range had blown out her crotch.

Fargo hurried outside in an attempt to quell the nausea welling up in his throat. He made it to the porch rail before vomiting. Shaking his head, he watched a buzzard pick in the foul-smelling upchuck.

Fargo cleared his throat and mouth of bile, then ambled to the bunkhouse. He discovered its thatched roof had been burned off and the length of its interior gutted by the fire. The body of a Mexican man lay sprawled facedown a few feet outside the only door in the bunkhouse. Inside, he found charred remains of six bodies. He presumed they were Mexicans also.

Walking back to the big house Fargo saw a well between it and an adobe barn. He angled for the well. As he lowered the water bucket, he looked around the area. Horses and mules stood watching him over the top rail of a corral behind a smaller adobe barn. A chicken coop stood alongside the barn. The chickens inside clucked that they were suffocating-hot. There was a high board fence behind the larger adobe structure. Fargo heard pigs grunting behind the fence. Fifty yards left of the house was a rather wide depression. The area between it and the house and barns had been cleared of all growth.

Fargo whistled to the Ovaro. He trotted around the house with his ears perked. After removing the canteens from the saddle horn, Fargo aimed the pinto toward the depression and slapped his rump. He watched until the thirsty stallion disappeared over the near edge of the ravine, then hauled the bucket of water up.

He drank first, then filled the canteens and poured the rest on top of his head. Temporarily refreshed, he started doing what had to be done.

First he went to the corral and set the horses and mules free. All ran straight to the depression. Then he opened the coop gate and chased the chickens outside. He moved to and looked over the top of the pig's pen. A sow hog and four shoats looked up at him. Their mud hole was bone-dry, baked to a cinder. He let them out. The sow immediately headed for the depression, her squealing brood chasing after her.

Fargo then turned to the sad task of burying the dead. He got a pick and a shovel out of the smaller building and dug two common graves near the well, from which he hauled up water to pour on the hard soil to soften it. Finished, he went to the bunkhouse, where he used partly burned timbers to lay the charred bodies on and dragged them to the grave. After all were in, he shoveled on the soil.

At the house, he used bed linens to drag the family to their grave. He lay the man and wife side by side, then lay the boy on top of his father and the girl atop her mother. He covered them with a sheet, then put the shovel to work.

Finished, he offered a brief prayer, then joined the Ovaro standing knee-deep in the narrow stream that flowed in the depression. Fargo washed his clothes and himself. Draping his gun belt over a shoulder, he took the wet clothing to the house and spread it over the porch rail to dry. Watching the sun go down from where he sat on the front steps, he ate a tin of beans he'd found in the pantry.

He whistled for the Ovaro. When the pinto came to him, Fargo removed the saddle and his other stuff. He put the saddle on the porch rail, his bedroll on the porch, and carried his Sharps and saddlebags upstairs to the front bedroom.

Slipping his Colt under a pillow, he lay on the first bed he'd seen in over a week and quickly found sleep.

Somebody shouting, "Hey! Anybody home?" jerked his eyes open. His gun hand instantly gripped the Colt. Bright moonlight spilled through the pair of open windows at the side of the bed.

He propped on one elbow and looked down and saw two lean riders. Cocking his Colt, he said, "Yeah. I'm coming down." He strapped the gun belt around his bare waist, holstered the cocked Colt, and went down to see what they wanted.

Standing two paces behind the screen door, Fargo sized up the pair. They appeared young and more like ranchhands than drifters. One wore chaps, both had Texas-style cowboy hats. Their hands rested on their pommels, well away from their holstered weapons. Fargo reckoned they were harmless enough, wranglers looking for work. He stepped onto the porch and asked, "What are you men doing here this time of night? Seems to me you could have waited within sight of the place till morning."

The one on Fargo's left shifted in his saddle and asked amusedly, "Pardon me for asking, mister, but do you always go 'round buck-assed naked at night?"

Clearing his throat, Fargo stepped to the rail and fetched his Levi's. Pulling them on, he answered, "Yes. There isn't anybody around to see me. What brings you way the hell out here?"

The one on Fargo's right answered in high-pitched drawl, "Mister, we're hongry as 'ol Billy Hell. Ain't had a bite to eat in nigh on three days. We couldn't wait for sunup."

Fargo could understand their having hunger pains. He motioned them inside, saying, "Come on in and I'll round up something for you to eat." Inside, he lit a lamp and led the way to the kitchen.

Sitting down at the table, they looked at the four place settings, then glanced questioningly at each other. Fargo saw their curious expressions and explained, "This isn't my place." He went on to say he'd stumbled onto the ranch earlier, found everybody murdered, and spent the rest of the day burying the bodies. Then he asked their names.

High-pitched answered, "Mine's Cooney Roberts."

Chaps said, "And I'm Hank Tyler. You are?"

"Skye Fargo."

"You a cowhand like me and Hank, here?" Cooney asked.

Fargo shook his head and started opening two tins of beans.

Hank asked, "What're you doing in this godforsaken part of Texas, anyhow? Where you headed?"

Fargo felt it best they didn't know he was headed for Austin to keep an appointment. The month-old message penned by State Senator David Winston was handed to him in Tucson by a Butterfield Line Overland Mail celerity stage driver. Winston made it brief: "Your presence at the state capitol in Austin, Texas, is most urgently requested. You shall receive $500 upon agreeing to accept a dangerous assignment that we will discuss when you arrive." Included in the envelope was $500 to cover Fargo's out-of-pocket expenses to get to Austin. Fargo still had $400 of the advance money tucked in his hip pocket. He answered, "I heard there was railroad work in Texas. Thought I'd look into it."

"I ain't heard about no railroad," Cooney said. "Have you?" He glanced at Hank.

"Nope," Hank offered. "Leastwise not in these parts."

Fargo was ready to move off the railroad subject. Again he inquired why they were here.

Hank finished off his plate of beans before muttering, "Oh, er, uh . . . Hell, Cooney, what is the name of that place anyhow? I forgot."

Cooney leaned back in his chair, sighed, and said, "Shitfire, Hank, I'm getting sick and tired of you saying, 'I forget,' all the time. Now, tell the man where we're going or I'm gonna bust you in the mouth."

Hank stared grim-jawed at Cooney for what

seemed an hour to Fargo before scooting his chair back and standing. Leaning over the table, Hank snarled, "Oh, yeah? Who's gonna help you, Cooney?"

Cooney hit him square in the mouth. Hank staggered back, shook his head, and dragged the back of his hand across his mouth. He looked at the blood on his hand, then squinted at Cooney. Fargo watched Hank check his teeth and the inside of his lips with his tongue as he balled his hands into fists. Hank was fast. He shot a right jab at Cooney's face and followed it with a left hook just as hard and fast. Cooney was faster. He ducked both fists.

Fargo moved back and gave them fighting room.

Hank took a hard blow in his abdomen that doubled him over. Then Cooney wound up and slammed an uppercut into Hank's jaw that straightened him up for the knockout. Cooney gritted his teeth and cocked his right hand to deliver it. Before he could move, Hank spit in his face and swung. Fargo learned Cooney had a glass jaw. It crunched and then Cooney's brown eyes crossed as he dropped to the floor, out cold.

Fargo handed the pail of water to the unsteady victor and asked, "Do you two always settle disputes with your knuckles?"

Hank rinsed out his mouth before answering, "Aw, Cooney's okay. A mite hot-tempered, that's all. Anyhow, I knew if I could get one lick in he'd crumble. Cooney, he can dish it out, but he can't take it. Got anyplace where we can sleep for the night? We'll be gone in the morning." He dumped the pail of water on Cooney's face.

Cooney stirred as Fargo said, "Up the stairs. Put your friend in one bedroom and yourself in the other. They're right across the hall from one an-

172

other. You might want to flop the girl's bloody mattress."

Fargo watched Hank lift Cooney's limp body and drape it over one shoulder. He smiled, "You want to show the way with the lamp?"

Fargo took him to the girl's room. Hank looked at the blood-soaked bed and said, "Goddamn, that's a whole lot of blood. Where'd you say he shot her, anyhow?"

"In the crotch," Fargo muttered.

Hank dumped Cooney faceup onto the bed. "He won't know the difference till daylight," Hank suggested dryly.

Fargo showed him the boy's room, then left him there and went to his own. He took off his gun belt but not his Levi's. As he returned the Colt to beneath his pillow, an uneasy feeling swept through Fargo. He lay down and drifted into sleep realizing neither Hank nor Cooney had said where they were going.

Shortly before dawn his wild-creature hearing alerted him to a soft sound. His eyes snapped opened instantly and his gun hand slipped under the pillow. Withdrawing his Colt, he thumbed back its hammer and listened for the sound that awakened him to come again. It did. One of them was creeping down the hall, coming to his door. The wooden floor squeaking betrayed the intruder.

Fargo sat up, faced the door, aimed at it, and waited. He watched the doorknob turn slowly.

He was applying pressure to the trigger when Hank's voice warned through a window screen behind him, "Shoot that Colt and you're a dead man."